Noreen knew her son needed a role model...

a man who would guide him, nurture him. A grandfather was nice, but every boy needed a father.

Her gaze went to Vinnie. Everything she heard about him told her he was exactly the opposite of what she and Billy needed, and yet she couldn't help the physical tug she felt when she looked at him.

Hormones, she decided. Sexual attraction. An incredible chemical reaction that started in her toes and ended in a ball of heat in the pit of her stomach.

She smiled as Vinnie pointed to her son, who'd been waving his hand madly to ask a question. Billy stood and smiled at Vinnie. "Hi. Remember me? You're gonna give my mommy a baby."

The innocent words seemed to echo throughout the school.

It seemed Billy already had his mind made up... but was Vinnie who she needed in her life?

Dear Reader,

August is jam-packed with exciting promotions and top-notch authors in Silhouette Romance! Leading off the month is RITA Award-winning author Marie Ferrarella with *Suddenly...Marriage!*, a lighthearted VIRGIN BRIDES story set in sultry New Orleans. A man and a woman, both determined to remain single, exchange vows in a mock ceremony during Mardi Gras, only to learn their bogus marriage is for real....

With over five million books in print, Valerie Parv returns to the Romance lineup with *Baby Wishes and Bachelor Kisses*. In this delightful BUNDLES OF JOY tale, a confirmed bachelor winds up sole guardian of his orphaned niece and must rely on the baby-charming heroine for daddy lessons—*and* lessons in love. Stella Bagwell continues her wildly successful TWINS ON THE DOORSTEP series with *The Ranger and the Widow Woman*. When a Texas Ranger discovers a stranded mother and son, he welcomes them into his home. But the pretty widow harbors secrets this lawman-in-love needs to uncover.

Carla Cassidy kicks off our second MEN! promotion with *Will You Give My Mommy a Baby?* A 911 call from a five-year-old boy lands a single mom and a true-blue, red-blooded hero in a sticky situation that quickly sets off sparks. *USA Today* bestselling author Sharon De Vita concludes her LULLABIES AND LOVE miniseries with *Baby and the Officer.* A crazy-about-kids cop discovers he's a dad, but when he goes head-to-head with his son's beautiful adoptive mother, he realizes he's fallen head over heels. And Martha Shields rounds out the month with *And Cowboy Makes Three*, the second title in her COWBOYS TO THE RESCUE series. A woman who wants a baby and a cowboy who needs an heir agree to marry but discover the honeymoon is just the beginning....

Don't miss these exciting stories by Romance's unforgettable storytellers!

Enjoy,

Joan Marlow Golan

Joan Marlow Golan
Senior Editor Silhouette Books

Please address questions and book requests to:
Silhouette Reader Service
U.S.: 3010 Walden Ave., P.O. Box 1325, Buffalo, NY 14269
Canadian: P.O. Box 609, Fort Erie, Ont. L2A 5X3

WILL YOU GIVE MY MOMMY A BABY?

Carla Cassidy

Silhouette
R O M A N C E™
Published by Silhouette Books
America's Publisher of Contemporary Romance

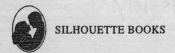

SILHOUETTE BOOKS

ISBN 0-373-19315-7

WILL YOU GIVE MY MOMMY A BABY?

Books by Carla Cassidy

CARLA CASSIDY

had her first Silhouette novel, *Patchwork Family*, published in September of 1991, and since that time she has written over twenty-five novels for five Silhouette lines. She's looking forward to writing many more books and bringing hours of pleasure to her readers.

OUT OF THE MOUTHS OF BABES...

Dear Mommy,

I want a baby brother. You told me that to get one you had to get married first. Well, what about if you marry Vinnie and make a baby brother with him?

Vinnie is a really nice guy. He would make a good daddy. He saves people and is a real hero. He likes to go camping. He likes to do three-legged races. He has good eyes and his whiskers grow really fast. He is awesome and I think we should marry him.

I promise I will be a good big brother. I will be like Vinnie and save my brother from ever getting hurt and I will be a hero, too. I will share my toys with him. And when he is scared, I will hold his hand.

I love you, Mommy, and if you do this, I promise I will be a good boy forever and ever.

Love,

Billy

Chapter One

Noreen Simmons heard the sirens above the sputter and growl of the old push lawn mower. She was used to the sound of sirens in the small town of Ridgeview, Kansas. A hospital was two blocks away from her home, and the local traffic patrolmen never missed an opportunity to blare their sirens while chasing down an errant speeder.

Noreen paused a moment as she mowed her lawn, eyeing the large yard still awaiting a manicure. If she'd been smart, she would have waited until later in the day when the sun had gone down. As it was, the relentless late-spring sun baked her bare shoulders, and perspiration trickled a ticklish path down the center of her back.

But later Billy wouldn't be napping. A smile curved her lips as she thought of her five-year-old son. If she waited until later, Billy would insist on helping, and a simple chore would become much more complicated and take twice as long.

She frowned as she realized the siren was growing louder. She pulled the lever to stop the mower, then walked around the side of the house to the front yard. Her eyes widened as a fire truck came into view up the block.

Frantically she looked up and down the street, seeking a swirl of smoke that would indicate trouble for one of her neighbors. Nothing. No dark cloud of smoke marred the perfect blue of the sky.

Then maybe it was a medical emergency. Her heart jumped in her throat as she thought of the elderly Emily Winston who lived two doors down. Mrs. Winston had already had two heart attacks, yet insisted on living alone.

Noreen breathed a sigh of relief as the old woman opened her door and stepped outside, looking frail, but not in need of emergency aid.

Suddenly the fire engine pulled to a halt in front of her own house, and half a dozen men jumped off, racing toward her. She recognized all the men but one. Most of them she'd known all her life.

"Michael, what's going on?" she asked the eldest man.

"We got a 911 call from here. You all right? Everything okay?" His gaze darted frantically back and forth between the house and her.

She nodded, then her heart dropped. "Billy!" she cried. She turned and ran toward the house, aware of pounding footsteps behind her.

She threw open the front door and raced into the

living room. Her son sat on the sofa like an innocent cherub. Right next to the telephone.

As Noreen crossed the room to her son, she was vaguely aware of several of the firemen coming into the house behind her. "Billy, did you call 911?" she asked as she crouched down at his side.

He nodded, an angelic smile lighting his face. Freckles dusted his turned-up nose, and his blue eyes danced as he said, "We learned about 911 in school. I called the firemen."

"Why, Billy? There's no fire," Noreen asked, embarrassed by the obvious false alarm.

"I want a baby brother. The other day Grandpa said firemen bring babies."

Noreen stared at her son, for a moment her mind whirling to make the connection. Then she remembered her father's conversation at dinner the night before and everything became crystal clear.

Her humiliation deepened as she stood and faced the three firemen who had followed her into the house. "I'm sorry, guys. It's a mistake, a false alarm."

Michael raked a hand through his gray hair, smiled and relaxed, the wrinkles in his weathered face easing. "Are you sure?"

"Positive."

"No harm done." Michael said. "It's been a slow week. I imagine the chief is on his way here. I'll contact the station and let them know we're clear."

Noreen walked out with the men, making a mental note to have a little discussion concerning the facts of life and the responsibilities of dialing 911 with her son. Drat her father and his penchant for old stories. This was all his fault.

She looked at the handsome firefighter she'd never seen before. "You must be new," she said, ignoring the faint flutter of her heart as she realized he was quite handsome.

"Oh, yeah, Vinnie here started two weeks ago," Michael explained. "Vinnie, this is Noreen Simmons. Noreen, Vinnie Pastorelli." After Michael made the introductions, he started back toward the fire truck, where several of the men had taken off their hats and sat down at the curb in the shade of a large oak tree.

Vinnie Pastorelli took her hand in his, his dark eyes sparkling as a flirtatious grin lifted the corners of his mouth. "Nice to meet you, Noreen."

Noreen had only met one man before in her life who had the ability to make her feel undressed beneath his gaze. Vinnie Pastorelli was the second. As his gaze swept down the length of her, an uncomfortable warmth suffused her. She wished her old cutoff shorts were just a little bit longer and the tank top just a little bigger.

"Nice to meet you, too," she replied. She pulled her hand from his, oddly reluctant to break the connection.

"I knew I was going to like it here. Ridgeview grows the prettiest women." He smiled. "I've always had a fondness for freckles." His gaze went to her bare shoulders, where she knew a few freckles had appeared from her time in the sun.

Apparently he had no idea who she was, otherwise he wouldn't be flirting so openly. It was kind of refreshing. She was accustomed to respect, a wary distance from the men in the department. And it had been so long since she'd practiced the art of flirting. She noted he wore no wedding band.

"So, where's home, Mr. Pastorelli?" she asked.

"Right now a rented room off Main Street. Two weeks ago home was Chicago. And please, call me Vinnie." Again his gaze caressed her, making her wish she wasn't hot and sweaty and clad in such skimpy clothing. She wished her hair wasn't swept into an untidy ponytail and her face devoid of makeup.

"Will you give my mommy a baby?"

Both Vinnie and Noreen jumped at the sound of Billy's voice. Vinnie laughed. "Sounds like fun, but your daddy might have a problem with that," he said.

"I don't have a daddy," Billy answered matter-of-factly. "So it's okay."

Noreen didn't think she could blush more. "Billy, have you cleaned your room like you were supposed to?"

"Yup." Billy grinned, his blue eyes sparkling with childish innocence.

"Why don't you go see if Michael will let you ring the bell on the engine," she said. He nodded and ran to Michael.

"Cute kid," Vinnie observed, but his gaze remained focused on her.

"Yeah, he doesn't know it yet, but he's going to get one major lecture when all of you leave." She felt a blush warm her face. "He has gotten it into his head that firemen deliver babies."

"Sometimes we do," he agreed. He looked over to where the other men seemed in no hurry to get back on the truck. Noreen assumed Michael had called the station to let them know they were free and ready to take a call should one come in.

As Vinnie looked back at her, once again she felt the heat his gaze evoked. Like a trailing finger against her back, an intimate touch inside her thigh, his gaze seemed to touch places that hadn't been touched in a very long time.

Noreen was pleased to feel the utterly feminine response. She'd thought that part of her died when Jesse had left four years ago.

"So," Vinnie said as he took a step closer to her, bringing with him a sweet scent of male, and an earthy spice cologne. "If your son doesn't have a father around, I guess that means you're a single parent."

"Yes, I am." She held her breath, unsure what she expected, but expectation winging through her nevertheless.

"If you ever have a fire, don't hesitate to call me to put it out." The gleam in his eyes told her he was aware of the double entendre.

Noreen winced. "That was really bad," she said.

He laughed, his reply lost beneath the wail of a siren approaching. They all turned to see the fire chief's car barreling down the street toward the house.

The car screeched to a halt, and a tall, big-boned man flew out of the passenger seat and hurried across the lawn toward Noreen and Vinnie.

Charlie O'Roark, fire chief for the Ridgeview Fire

Department, looked like a poster ad for Irish firefighters. With a bush of red hair and the brawn of a potato farmer, he looked as if he'd be right at home in a Dublin pub. However, the closest he'd ever gotten to his motherland was a nip of Irish coffee on special occasions.

As Charlie wrapped her in a bear hug, Vinnie's eyes widened in surprise. "Criminy, when I heard that the call came in from this address, I think my heart stopped beating for a minute." He released her and stepped back. "What happened?"

"Billy called 911," Noreen explained. "He wanted the firemen to bring him a baby brother."

Charlie stared at her for a long moment, then threw back his head and roared with laughter. "Ah, that kid is a pip."

Noreen scowled. "It's all your fault. You and your firemen stories." She grinned, unable to sustain any real anger. "I'm sorry we scared you," she said.

He reached up and softly touched her cheek. "Scared the hell out of me." He cleared his throat, for the first time looking at Vinnie. "Pastorelli, have you met my one and only?"

Vinnie looked as if his collar had suddenly grown too tight. Noreen realized Vinnie had no idea of their relationship. She had a feeling Vinnie was suddenly sweating the fact that he might have been flirting with the chief's girlfriend.

"Yes, sir, we met." He shot Noreen a nervous glance, obviously wondering if she intended to say anything about his flagrant flirting.

She decided to let him off the hook. "Vinnie was just making sure everything was all right, Dad."

Vinnie relaxed somewhat and shot her a smile that warmed her to her toes. Good grief, she thought, the man's smile should be registered as a lethal weapon.

"Pastorelli. Let's go," Michael called from the truck as the motor roared to life.

"It was nice meeting you, Noreen. I'll see you around." He backed up, his smile still spilling heat through her.

She found herself foolishly returning his smile for a moment. Then she watched as he climbed into the engine, and the big vehicle lumbered down the street.

Turning back to her father, she saw a frown wrinkling his forehead. "What's wrong?"

"Don't you be getting any ideas about Vinnie Pastorelli," he said.

She stared at him in surprise. "What are you talking about? I just met the man."

"He's a good-looking single man, and I saw the way he was looking at you and you were looking at him." Charlie threw an arm around her shoulder. "He's a player, honey. Not what you and Billy need in your lives."

An odd disappointment swept through Noreen. A player. Of course. His eyes had held the same magnetic quality as her ex-husband, Jesse. And Jesse had been the ultimate player. She smiled at her dad. "Don't worry. I'm not about to repeat past mistakes."

She looked over to where Billy was digging in the flower bed, where she'd intended to plant flowers.

The space now sprouted a colorful array of dump trucks and pickups. Billy had commandeered the spot as a perfect road for his assortment of miniature vehicles.

Jesse might have been her mistake, but she could never regret the product of their brief marriage. Billy was her heart, the only male in her life other than her father for the past four years.

"We still on for dinner tonight?" Her father interrupted her thoughts.

She smiled up at him. "Unless you have other plans."

He snorted. "What plans would I have? A grizzled old bear like me?" He kissed her forehead. "I'll see you at six."

Noreen watched her father get back in his car and drive off. Unburdened by his presence, her thoughts instantly went back to Vinnie Pastorelli.

For that brief moment when Vinnie had flirted with her, she'd felt deliciously female. She'd experienced that breathless anticipation, the instinctive flush of being attracted to a man and knowing the feeling was reciprocated. It had been a heady moment…and a fleeting one.

A player. A lady's man. A man who would be unable to understand the word commitment. The last thing she needed in her life.

"Yoo-hoo." Emily Winston waved to Noreen as she stepped off her front porch and walked the short distance to where Noreen stood. "Everything all right, dear?"

"Fine," Noreen replied. "Last night at dinner my

dear father told an old story about delivering a baby, and Billy got it into his head that firemen bring babies, so he called 911.''

Emily laughed, fine lines dancing out from her bright blue eyes. She looked at the little boy, who pushed a cement truck along a rut in the dirt. ''He's a good boy.''

''Yes, he is. I'm not sure who should get my lecture, Billy or my father. I thought about making Dad explain the facts of life to Billy, but then I remembered the malarkey he told me when I was young.''

''The stork?'' Emily asked in amusement.

''Worse…the cabbage patch. It took my mother months to straighten me out.''

The women laughed, and Noreen asked how her neighbor was doing. ''You feeling okay?''

She nodded. ''Fine, dear, just fine. I'm being careful, doing everything the doctors tell me to do. And now I'd better get back inside where it's cool.'' With a dainty wave, she turned and went back to her house.

Noreen watched her go, affection swelling her heart for the woman who'd been such a support when Jesse had left. For days after his abandonment, Emily Winston had brought over chocolate cake, brownies and fudge, as if an overload of chocolate could heal a broken heart.

The only thing the treats had done was add five pounds to Noreen's thighs and make her face blotchy.

''Hey, slugger,'' she said as she sat down on the porch next to where Billy played. ''We need to have a little talk about the telephone and babies.'' As her son joined her on the porch, she shoved all thoughts of the handsome, sexy Vinnie Pastorelli from her mind.

"As always, a wonderful dinner." Charlie pushed aside his empty plate and pulled his coffee cup closer.

Noreen smiled at her father. "It's hard to mess up hamburgers."

"Ah, you'd be surprised. I remember the time your mother grilled burgers outside. They were the hardest, blackest things I'd ever seen." His smile wavered slightly, as it always did when he spoke of Noreen's mother.

Noreen touched his hand lightly, then stood and began to clear the table. Her mother had passed away the same summer that Jesse had left.

It had been a summer of heartache, of loss. There were times when the smells of fresh-cut grass and barbecue fires caused a spasm of grief to possess her.

"So, how are things down at the station?" she asked, knowing talk of work always raised her father's spirits.

As Charlie chattered about the men, the condition of the station, the lack of funds for the department, Noreen cleaned up the dishes.

It was a nightly ritual—Charlie ate dinner with them and stayed until Billy's bedtime, then left to go home. It was a comfortable routine, the sharing of the lonely hours between work and sleep.

"It's too early to say how Pastorelli is going to work in an actual situation. We haven't had a fire since he arrived in town."

Noreen's ears pricked up at the mention of the

handsome firefighter. "I understand he's from Chicago. I wonder what brought him to a little town like Ridgeview, Kansas?" She rejoined her father at the table.

"Who knows? The man came with a good recommendation, although he's only been a firefighter for a little over a year."

Noreen looked at her father in surprise. She would have guessed Vinnie to be in his late twenties, early thirties. "What was he doing before this?"

"I'm not sure...a lawyer I think."

Again surprise swept through her. Why on earth would a man who had a law degree decide to become a civil servant in a dirty, dangerous job with far too little compensation?

"Now get that look off your face," Charlie said.

"What look?"

"You're interested in him. I see the wheels turning in your head. I don't want you to get tangled up with Vinnie Pastorelli," he said firmly. He reached across the table and took her hand in his. "Honey, I want the best for you and Billy. You don't need another fly-by-night man in your life. Vinnie has only been in town two weeks, and I swear he already knows half the single women in the four-county area. Besides," he took another sip of his coffee, then continued, "his former chief said although he's a good fireman, he has a bit of a tendency to be a hotdogger."

Noreen frowned. Of all the occupations where being a hotdogger could be hazardous, firefighting was one of the leading ones. A man who took unnecessary chances, men who threw caution to the wind, often ended up badly hurt…or worse, putting the other men who worked with him at risk.

"Well, I think I'd better take off. I've got to get back to the station." Charlie finished his coffee and stood. "Where's that grandson of mine?"

"In his room, hopefully getting ready for bed." Noreen looked at the clock, surprised to discover it was after eight. She still had papers to grade before the night was over.

As her dad went into Billy's room to say goodnight, Noreen added their coffee cups to the other dirty dishes in the dishwasher.

Kitchen clean, she went into the living room. She opened her briefcase and pulled out the second-grade math papers.

She'd graded four by the time her dad returned from Billy's room. "Don't get up," he said as she started to rise from the sofa. "I'll see you tomorrow, sweets."

She smiled warmly. "'Night, Dad."

It wasn't until much later, after Billy had been tucked in for the night and her papers had all been graded, that Noreen thought of Vinnie Pastorelli once again.

She poured herself a glass of iced tea and took it out to the front porch. Sitting down on the porch swing, she thought of the way Vinnie's dark eyes had glittered, as if he knew the gift of laughter and the power of passion.

Frowning, she took a sip of the iced tea, enjoying the cold liquid as it slid down her throat. The last thing she needed or wanted in her life was another man like Jesse, a man who promised the world with his eyes…to each and every woman he met.

Jesse had been the ultimate player in a game Noreen refused to play…the game of betrayal, of heartbreak and broken vows. And according to her father, Vinnie Pastorelli was cut from the same cloth.

Too bad. Noreen would like to find a man to date. She hoped eventually to fall in love again and give Billy a real father.

Settling back in the swing, she was filled with a wistful longing as the scent of the summer night wrapped around her. There were moments when her loneliness seemed overwhelming. She wanted somebody to share her life with, somebody to depend on and love.

Yes, it would be nice to fall in love again, to share secrets, hopes and dreams. But the next time she would be smarter. She wouldn't allow herself to get caught up in passion, in believing empty lies and false promises. Next time she would be certain the man understood commitment.

She sighed. Despite her thoughts to the contrary, she had a feeling her dreams that night just might be of flames, and heat…and Vinnie Pastorelli putting out her fire.

Chapter Two

"Come on, Lieutenant, there's got to be somebody else who can do it." Vinnie looked anxiously at gray-haired Michael Walters.

Michael shook his head. "It's not a matter of somebody else doing it. It's assigned to you." He grinned at Vinnie. "The new guy *always* gets the school job."

Vinnie's gut roiled. School. School meant children. Little boys and girls with sweet youthful faces and the scent of childhood.

He looked at Michael, wondering if one more protest would do any good. He decided by Michael's expression it wouldn't. "So, what do I have to do?"

Michael reared back in his chair. "Be at the Ridgeview Elementary School at three o'clock. You'll be talking to a group of kindergarten, first- and second-graders. Give them the usual fire safety tips, tell them how great it is to be a firefighter, and for goodness' sake, don't look like that, as if I'm sending you into a burning building alone. Now get out of here. It must be lunchtime. The smell of Rogers's chili has been making my mouth water all morning.''

Vinnie left Michael's office and headed for the station's kitchen area, his stomach rebelling at the thought of yet another day of Sam Rogers's home-style chili. But Vinnie wouldn't complain. In the three weeks that he'd been a member of the Ridgeview Fire Department, Sam had been the friendliest of the twelve firefighters.

Vinnie suspected it was because he and Sam were about the same age, and Sam, married with two children, had decided to take Vinnie under his wing and get him married like the rest of them.

Of course Sam knew nothing about Vinnie's past, about the tragedy that had changed his life and made it impossible for him to ever entertain the notion of love or marriage again.

Entering the kitchen, Vinnie grinned at Sam, who stirred a vat of the strong-smelling chili. "There's my man," Sam exclaimed. "Where have you been?"

"Talking to Lieutenant Walters." Vinnie slid onto a stool at the counter where the men usually sat to eat. "I'm supposed to go to the elementary school this afternoon and give the kids a thrill." His tone relayed his enthusiasm for the assignment.

Sam laughed. "Hey, be grateful it's the elementary school. Those kids are still impressionable enough to believe we're all heroes. Now, the high school kids…that's another story, another species of humans.''

Vinnie laughed, and Sam winked at him. "Besides,

some of those teachers are single and attractive. Unlike my first-grade teacher, who had a mustache healthier than my father's and always smelled of mothballs.'' Sam stopped stirring his concoction. ''You know the chief's daughter is a second-grade teacher.''

''She is?'' For the first time the glimmer of a silver lining lifted Vinnie's spirits.

He could visualize Noreen perfectly, with her chestnut hair escaping the confines of a ponytail and her freckles dancing atop her shoulders as if begging to be kissed.

''Don't even think about it,'' Sam advised, as if he could read Vinnie's mind. ''Unless you want to spend your time here in the doghouse, you'll steer clear of Noreen Simmons.''

''The chief is a little protective of his daughter?''

Sam smiled. ''Like King Kong is just a little bit monkey.'' Sam picked up his ladle and stirred the chili once again. ''Besides, Noreen doesn't date, and I thought you were dating Suzie Peterson.''

''One date. Suzie and I had one date.'' Vinnie frowned. ''She was nice, but she just seemed so...so—''

''Eager?'' Sam laughed. ''I think Suzie's mother told her she'd turn into a pumpkin if she wasn't married by thirty. Suzie's twenty-nine and counting.''

''Yeah, I thought I sensed a desperation when she began talking about what beautiful children we'd have and we hadn't even finished our first meal together.'' Vinnie smiled and shook his head. ''She grew decidedly more cool when I told her I wasn't in the market for a wife.''

Sam grinned knowingly. "Sooner or later you'll change your tune. You'll meet a woman who will knock your socks off, and you'll be whistling the wedding-bell blues until the lovely lady takes pity on you and marries you.''

Vinnie laughed and shook his head. "No way, my man. There's not a woman alive who has the capacity to make me want to waltz down the aisle.''

"Hey, Rogers, that chili ready yet?" Several other men walked into the kitchen, effectively halting the conversation between Vinnie and Sam.

It wasn't until later that afternoon, as Vinnie drove toward the Ridgeview Elementary School, that he found himself thinking about the conversation.

Sam was wrong. Vinnie had told him the truth when he'd said there was no woman alive who could make him want to marry. Sam couldn't know that Vinnie's heart, which had once beat with love and passion, with hopes and dreams, now was dead, buried beneath the ashes of the past and the dreadful ache of loss.

He pulled into the school parking lot and looked at his watch. He had fifteen minutes before he had to go in and face a roomful of kids. Dread roared through him as he stared at the one-story brick building and imagined all the children inside.

It wasn't that he disliked children. He'd once loved the idea of a houseful of kids, of early-morning snuggling and bedtime stories. He remembered straw-berry-scented bubble bath and little hair barrettes the color of a bright blue crayon. Lullabies sung in a sweet voice and night-lights keeping monsters at bay.

Funny, the pain that accompanied these memories wasn't as intense as it used to be…more like the lingering echo of what once had been.

He got out of his car, irritated with his thoughts, his memories. He'd put the past behind him, started a new life that had no room for memories.

He reached into the back seat and pulled out the large duffle bag containing handouts and visual aids. He could do this. He could look out into a sea of children's faces and not feel anything.

Despite this assurance to himself, he felt a cold bead of sweat working its way down the side of his face and knew it wasn't the heat, but nerves, that caused the perspiration. Silly to feel so nervous about a roomful of kids. As he approached the school door, he sucked in a mouthful of confidence and charged forward.

The secretary greeted him as he walked into the office and took him immediately to the gymnasium, where six classes of children awaited him.

Excitement swirled in the air as the kids giggled and shouted back and forth and teachers admonished and clapped their hands for order.

Vinnie spotted Noreen immediately. She stood next to the opposite wall, talking softly to a young boy with a belligerent look on his face.

Noreen looked much different today than she had a week ago. Her hair was neatly coiled in an attractive braid down her back, and the enticing freckles were hidden beneath a pale pink blouse that highlighted the coppery glints in her chestnut hair. A gray skirt and high heels emphasized the length and shapeliness of her legs.

As he followed the secretary to the front of the gym, his gaze remained focused on Noreen. She finished speaking to the boy, whose truculent expression transformed to a shy smile. She pointed him to a spot on the floor, patted him on the back, then looked up.

Her gaze met Vinnie's. A smile curved her generous mouth upward. Warmth burst through him. He felt as if he were a gawky fifteen-year-old and the head cheerleader had just smiled at him.

However, he wasn't fifteen. He was thirty-two, far too old for a teenage crush. Sam had said that Noreen didn't date. Vinnie wondered why? She was a fine-looking woman and surely could have her pick of the town's eligible bachelors.

The taste of challenge replaced the nervousness he'd felt moments before. He was one hell of a fireman, and he'd give a program to knock the socks off these kids. Then he'd see if he couldn't perhaps make Noreen think twice about her nondating policy.

Noreen watched him with interest. She didn't care about the words he said, the information he shared. She'd cut her teeth on fire safety and the inner workings of the department. There was next to nothing Vinnie could say that she hadn't heard a hundred times before.

She'd sensed a little nervousness when he'd first begun speaking, and somehow that had been attractive. As he continued, and the kids responded enthusiastically, he'd relaxed, confidence reappearing in the gleam of his dark eyes, the straight set of his broad shoulders, and that had been even more attractive to her.

His dark hair shone beneath the artificial lights, looking silky and thick. Character lines etched his slender face, lines that spoke of laughter...and perhaps a touch of heartache. But it was his eyes that captured her attention. They danced with liveliness, with a sense of mirth mingling with a dash of arrogance.

She averted her gaze from him, irritated that it was always the men all wrong for her that she was attracted to. The bad boys, the men who stuttered in fear at the word *commitment*. Men like Jesse, who'd filled her days with laughter and her nights with passion, but had run at the first hint of responsibility and real daily adult life.

Instead, she focused her attention on her students, pleased by how well behaved they were as they listened attentively.

She looked toward the front of the gym, where the kindergartners sat, instantly able to pick out Billy from the group. His hair sparkled with the coppery glints of a new penny, and she could see his excitement as he listened to Vinnie.

There was only one thing Billy loved more than the idea of being a fireman, and that was his grandfather, the fireman.

Billy had no memory of his father. Jesse had left when Billy was only twenty-four months old, far too young to have stored any memories of the man who'd fathered him.

Noreen knew Billy needed a role model, a man who would be willing to take on the responsibility of guiding him, nurturing him. A grandfather was nice, but every boy needed a father.

And Noreen wanted somebody in her life, a man to hold her through the night, listen to her hopes, her fears. A man who could fill the yawning emptiness she sometimes felt just before sleep, take away the loneliness that Jesse had left behind.

But she refused to dance an array of men through Billy's life, allowing the little boy to form attachments to men who eventually turned out all wrong for the role of father. It was easier, safer to remain alone.

Her gaze went back to Vinnie, now answering questions from the kids who raised their hands. Everything she'd heard about him told her he was exactly the opposite of what she and Billy needed, and yet she couldn't help the physical tug she felt when she looked at him.

Hormones, she decided. Sexual attraction. A perverse chemical reaction that started in her toes and ended in a ball of heat in the pit of her stomach. Yes, he was nice to look at, but definitely not what she and Billy needed in their lives.

She smiled as Vinnie pointed to her son, who'd been waving his hand madly to ask a question. Billy stood and smiled at Vinnie. "Hi. Remember me? You're gonna give my mommy a baby."

The innocent words seemed to ring and echo throughout the gymnasium. Some of the kids tittered, and Noreen felt her face flame bright. Vinnie's mouth worked, but nothing came out. Billy's kindergarten teacher came to the rescue, quickly asking the students to thank Vinnie for his time.

"Hey, girlfriend, you been holding out on me?" Cindy Walker, a first-grade teacher and Noreen's best friend, sidled up beside her as the kids all clapped to show their appreciation of the program.

"Where did you meet that hunk, and when did you decide he should make a baby with you?"

Noreen rolled her eyes. "I met him last week when Billy decided to call 911. He wanted a baby brother. Trust me, it's a long story, and the bottom line is there's nothing to tell."

"So you aren't going to make babies with him?"

"Not hardly." Again a blush warmed Noreen's cheeks.

Cindy looked at Vinnie, who was walking out of the gymnasium, then back to Noreen. "Even if you don't actually make a baby with him, I imagine practicing would be fun."

Noreen elbowed her friend in the ribs. Cindy chuckled, then gazed at Noreen, her dark eyes warm with friendship. "Seriously, hon. It's time you started dating again. Time you learn how to trust again."

Noreen was saved from having to answer by the bell ringing, announcing the end of the school day. Pandemonium broke out as the kids rushed to line up for their buses, and teachers attempted to break up the usual pushing and shoving that took place in the daily process. The kids had been unusually rambunctious lately with summer vacation only a week away.

Fifteen minutes later, after seeing Billy off to day care, Noreen sank down at her desk in her classroom. The room always seemed odd at this time of day, uncharacteristically silent and yet haunted by the remaining echoes of giggles and chattering of little children.

She kicked her shoes off beneath the desk and rubbed her feet together, wishing she were already home and in a pair of shorts instead of wearing dress clothes, hose and high heels.

Eyeing the stack of pictures she'd had the students draw that afternoon, she decided to hang them on the strip of corkboard that was just below the ceiling of the room. She dragged her chair out from behind the desk and into one corner. By standing on tiptoes and stretching her full height, she could just manage to insert thumbtacks to hold the pictures in place.

Whoever had designed the rooms with the corkboard so high must have been a sadist, she thought. Still, she loved the way the room looked, decorated with the students' colorful creativity.

"Looks like fun."

The deep, familiar voice created a wealth of warmth inside her. She whirled around on the chair, nearly losing her balance, to see Vinnie standing in the classroom doorway. She grabbed the back of the chair to steady herself.

"You have an odd definition of fun," she returned, irritated that by his mere presence he could make her feel flustered. "What can I do for you, Mr. Pastorelli?" She turned back around and hung another picture.

"You could join me in an after-work cup of coffee."

"Thank you, but I don't think so." She turned to look at him once again. "I really don't...you know...do that."

A dark eyebrow danced up in amusement. "You don't drink coffee? Okay, we'll make it iced tea or lemonade."

"No, that's not what I mean. I drink coffee. I don't date."

"But this isn't a date." He leaned against the doorjamb, a lazy smile curving his sensual lips. "If it were a date, I'd pick you up at your house, we'd go out to dinner, then maybe dancing or to see a movie. Then I'd take you back home, trying to decide if I dare kiss you good-night or not."

He frowned, the twinkling of his eyes belying the gesture. "Having coffee with the new guy in town isn't against your religion, is it?"

Despite her desire not to, Noreen laughed. "No, it's not against my religion," she replied.

"Great! Then where are we going to have a cup of coffee?"

Although all her instincts told her to run in the other direction, Noreen's common sense told her she was making far too much out of the situation. After all, it was just a quick cup of coffee. She looked at her watch. She had just a little over an hour before she usually picked up Billy from his after-school day care.

"Of course, I could suggest my place," he said with a devilish glint in his eyes.

"And be drinking that coffee alone," she retorted.

He laughed, obviously amused rather than insulted by her quick reply. "Then how about my second choice of location...the Ridgeview Café?"

"Okay. I've got to finish up here. Why don't I meet you there in about fifteen minutes?"

"You've got a date," he replied. "Oops, I mean I'll see you there." He grinned, then turned on his heels and disappeared from the doorway.

It's just coffee, Noreen told herself as she finished hanging the last of the pictures. But she knew it was more than that. It was a first foray into the uncharted territory of social interaction with a member of the opposite sex.

Jesse had been gone for four years, and in that time she'd never spent any time alone with a man other than her son and her father.

She was twenty-six years old and had married at nineteen. She hadn't had a lot of experience dating before her marriage.

She retrieved her shoes from beneath the desk and grabbed her purse and briefcase. She left her room and walked down the long hallway, her heels echoing in the quiet of the building. When she reached Cindy's classroom, she poked her head inside and spied her friend at her desk. "We still on for pizza tomorrow night?" It was tradition for the two friends and their sons to spend Friday nights together. Cindy's husband, Adam, was a doctor, who worked late hours in a clinic on Friday nights.

Cindy gave her a thumbs-up sign. "I'll pick you and Billy up about six. Oh, and Jeffrey wanted Billy to spend the night. If that's all right with you, pack him some pajamas and extra clothes and I'll bring him home Saturday morning.''

''It's fine with me,'' Noreen replied, then with a quick wave she headed out of the building. The humid heat slapped her in the face as she walked outside. It was the last week of May and already it felt like July or August. It promised to be a long, hot summer.

She got behind the wheel of her car and fought the impulse to drive straight to the day care, forget Vinnie Pastorelli and his invitation.

But she wouldn't do that. She'd told Vinnie she'd be there, and Noreen wasn't one to simply leave somebody hanging. Besides, it irritated her that a mere cup of coffee with the handsome newcomer in town would so fill her with anxiety.

She could handle herself, be friendly, but not overly so.

It might just be nice if she'd just allow herself to relax a little bit.

She drew a deep breath, then loosened her grip on the steering wheel. Maybe Cindy was right. It was time she started dating again. She'd been alone for too long. Of course, she would never date Vinnie. What little she'd heard about him made him a bad bet for any long-term relationship, and Noreen would consider nothing less.

She'd settled with Jesse, believing she could love him hard enough, long enough to change him. She was no longer an idealistic fool. She was no longer interested in a man she'd have to change, have to convince to be true to her.

Pulling into the Ridgeview Café, she tried to shove the last of her doubts behind. She looked at her watch. Thirty minutes before she would need to leave and pick up Billy. Nothing earth shattering could happen in the space of thirty minutes.

As she got out of her car, she suddenly thought of those coffee commercials, the ones with the attractive couple who'd found each other over a famous brand of coffee.

"Not in this lifetime," she muttered to herself. And not with Vinnie Pastorelli.

Chapter Three

Noreen spied him the moment she walked in. Vinnie sat in a booth near the back of the café. He motioned to her, that drop-dead gorgeous smile flashing at her like a neon welcome sign.

She relaxed somewhat as the familiar ambience of the café washed over her. She occasionally dropped by here after school with teacher friends, and once a week she, her father and Billy came here to eat dinner. She was grateful Vinnie had chosen the café, where she felt comfortable and knew most of the people who frequented the place.

Winding her way through the tables, she was conscious of Vinnie's gaze on her as she approached where he sat. He stood as she slid into the booth opposite him. "Did you get your pictures all hung?" he asked as he sat back down.

She nodded. "The kids love to see their artwork on display."

"I always preferred mine hidden away in some drawer," he replied. "I discovered early on that my natural talents in the art department were dismally lacking."

The conversation halted as the waitress appeared at their table. "Hi, Noreen...Vinnie. What can I get for the two of you?" Although Sarah Jensen tried to hide her surprise at seeing Noreen with Vinnie, she didn't quite mask the curiosity that gleamed from her eyes.

"Just coffee," Noreen replied, nodding to the pot Sarah held.

"Make it two," Vinnie added.

Sarah poured the drinks, then left them, casting Noreen one last glance of curiosity.

"You come in here pretty often?" Noreen asked.

"Most evenings that I'm not at the station, I have my dinner here." He grinned. "I cook as well as I draw."

Noreen laughed and felt the last of her tension drain away. "So, are you finding Ridgeview to your liking?" she asked as she added cream and sugar to her coffee. She tried to ignore how his blue uniform shirt emphasized the attractive olive cast to his skin and deepened the darkness of his eyes.

"It's a wonderful small town, the kind of place where I always wanted to live. A nice change of pace from Chicago."

"I would imagine fighting fires is far different from being a lawyer," she said.

His dark brows danced up, and he leaned back in the booth. "Why, Noreen, I do believe you've been checking up on me." He gave her a sinful, flirtatious grin.

A blush warmed her cheeks. The man was positively incorrigible. "Don't flatter yourself," she retorted. "I was trapped in an elevator, and two people were talking about you. I couldn't escape the conversation."

He laughed, the deep, rich sound causing a flutter of pleasure in Noreen's tummy. "So tell me, Noreen Simmons, what sort of natural talents do you have besides a penchant for deadly wit?"

Noreen paused a moment to take a sip of her coffee, trying to figure out how this man had managed to keep her so off balance in the mere minutes she'd spent with him. Was it only because she hadn't indulged in a conversation with a handsome man for so long?

She took another sip, thinking of his question. "I'm a good teacher, but I'm not sure if that's a natural talent or a learned skill."

"Probably a little of both. You like it?" He leaned forward, his gaze intent, as if her words were of great importance. She instantly recognized that this was probably one of his charms, the ability to make the woman he was with feel as if she was the most important person in his life.

"I love it," she answered without hesitation. "Working with kids is so rewarding and second-graders are especially wonderful. They are no longer babies, but still retain an innocence, an unself-consciousness that is delightful. Not a day goes by that I don't teach something...and learn something in return from the kids.''

She flushed and smiled shyly. ''Sorry, I tend to get a little carried away when I talk about work.''

''No, please don't apologize. I find your enthusiasm quite appealing.''

''You aren't enthusiastic about your work?'' she asked.

His light, easy smile faded beneath an expression of dark determination. ''*Enthusiastic* isn't exactly the right word. *Committed* would be more like it.''

He stared into his coffee cup for a long moment, and when he looked back up at her a veil of shadows subdued the sparkle of his eyes. ''Obsessed is even closer to the truth.'' He cleared his throat. ''Are you going to the picnic a week from Saturday?''

Noreen nodded, knowing he was referring to the firemen's picnic that was held once a year. The firefighters and all their families got together for a day of fun on the mayor's property just outside of town. ''I think my father would disown me if we didn't show up. It's sort of a family tradition.''

She looked at him for a long moment, the darkness in his eyes still there. ''What made you choose to move to Ridgeview?''

He blinked, the shadows unable to sustain their darkness beneath the flirtatious light that once again danced in his eyes. ''Somebody told me that if I took a job here in Ridgeview, one day the prettiest woman in town would have coffee with me at the local diner.''

Noreen didn't look away from his direct gaze. "Is that a skill or a natural talent?"

"What?"

"The flirting. The charming one-liners you throw out with such ease."

He stared at her in surprise, then threw his head back and laughed. Again warmth swept through Noreen at the pleasant, utterly masculine sound. "Ah, Noreen, I should have known you'd be a straight shooter."

She shrugged. "My father taught me to be wary of men who sweet-talk as easily as they breathe." A warning she'd studiously ignored in the case of Jesse.

"Somehow that doesn't surprise me. Your father doesn't seem the type to sweet-talk anyone."

Noreen smiled at thoughts of her dad. "You didn't answer my question."

He frowned a moment. "Oh, you mean talent or skill? Definitely a combination of both. My mother insists that the moment I was born I winked at the nurse and I've been a flirtatious fool ever since. I, however, maintain it was a conditioned survival response to having three older sisters."

"What about your father? Was he a flirting fool, too?"

"I don't know. My dad passed away when I was four,"

"Oh, I'm sorry."

He shook his head to dismiss her offer of sympathy. "I don't have many memories of him, but the few I have are quite pleasant. I think he was a good man." His lips curved upward once again. "And probably a flirting fool."

Noreen looked at her watch, mindful of the time.

"You have a plane to catch?" he asked teasingly.

"No, a son to pick up from day care."

"Ah, yes, the kid who insists we're going to make babies together." Vinnie leaned forward once again, the scent of his cologne eddying in the air and swirling around Noreen. "It's a tough job. May take us months of trying before we're successful."

She gave him a look of mock surprise. "I would have thought a man as capable, as confident, as you would be successful the very first time."

Vinnie's grin didn't falter. "You aren't really sure if you like me or not, are you?" He held up a hand before she could answer. "It's all right. I'm told I grow on people."

"Like fungus?"

He laughed again. "I like you, Noreen." His laughter faded and he gazed at her, his expression serious. "Why don't you have dinner with me tomorrow night?"

"I can't. I have a pizza engagement with a five-year-old. Besides, I told you I don't date."

"I intend to change that."

Noreen's heart thundered at the certainty of his words. She smiled, ignoring the quickening of her heartbeat and stood. "Good luck." She threw a dollar on the table to cover the cost of her coffee. "See you around, Pastorelli."

She made it all the way to the door without looking back, somehow knowing he expected her to give him one last glance. She could feel the heat of his gaze on her, watching her as she made her way to the front of the café. At the door she darted a quick look back at him. He nodded at her, that sexy smile lighting up his features.

A helpless bubble of laughter slid from her throat. The man was utterly incorrigible. And it both irritated and amused her that she found him a bundle of natural charm and skillful baloney.

As she picked up Billy from day care, all thoughts of Vinnie were lost beneath the childish chatter of her son. As they drove home he told her about his day, filling her in on everything a five-year-old found wonderful.

"How come I don't have a daddy?" Billy asked as Noreen pulled into the driveway.

Noreen turned off the engine and turned to look at her son. He'd never asked about his father before, never seemed to notice the absence in his life. She'd known eventually he'd want to know about the man who'd fathered him, known eventually she'd have to explain.

But how did she explain Jesse? How did she explain to a child that his daddy hadn't wanted him? Somehow it seemed easier to explain death than desertion.

"Honey, your daddy went away when you were a baby. He went far away to find work." Noreen didn't tell Billy that the last time she'd heard, Jesse was in California living with some wealthy older woman and sporting a surfboard and a handsome tan.

"And he's never coming back?" Billy's blue eyes

gazed at her earnestly. Noreen was relieved that she saw no deep sadness there, just a child trying to understand the vagarious nature of adults.

"No, honey. I don't think he's ever coming back." She unfastened her seat belt and reached across to stroke back a strand of his coppery hair from his forehead.

Billy frowned thoughtfully. "Can we get another one? One that will live with us and take me fishing and play catch and tell me stories at night?"

Noreen laughed, relaxing somewhat as she realized Billy could so easily replace one dad with another. Hopefully he would never feel the heart pain that she did at Jesse's abandonment. "We'll see. When I marry again, that man will be your new daddy."

"And he'll give us a new baby?"

"Let's not worry about a new baby right now." Noreen opened her car door and got out. "Grandpa will be here in an hour or so, and I need to get something started for supper."

"Okay." Together mother and son walked up the walk to the front door. "But, Mom...?"

"What, honey?" Noreen worked the key to unlock the door.

"Will you try to get married and give me a new daddy by the time I'm six?"

Again Noreen laughed. "I don't think so, honey. You'll be six next month and it takes more time than that to get married." And it helps if there's a man involved, Noreen thought.

Minutes later, with Billy playing in the backyard, Noreen browned sirloin strips for stroganoff. As the beef sizzled in the skillet, she found herself thinking of Vinnie once again.

Sizzle. The man had plenty of that. Sex appeal oozed from his pores. That, combined with a sense of humor and a touch of dangerous charm made him a deadly combination, and Noreen knew she would be smart to steer clear.

She'd felt the same way about Jesse. He'd charmed her with his words, thrilled her with his touch. She'd fallen for him hook, line and sinker. Although she'd known before they got married that Jesse was a ladies' man, she'd believed their marriage vows meant Jesse's sex appeal and charm belonged to her alone. What a laugh.

A knock on the front door pulled her from her thoughts. "Noreen, dear."

Noreen recognized the voice. Emily Winston. "In the kitchen, Emily," she answered.

The petite, white-haired woman walked into the kitchen, a covered pie tin in hand. "I did a little baking this morning and remembered you said your father's favorite was cherry pie." She set the tin on the table and removed the lid to display a thick, golden-crusted pie.

"Oh, Emily, how sweet." Noreen smiled fondly at the older woman. "Why don't you join us for supper? I'm making beef stroganoff and there's plenty, and Dad should be here within a half an hour."

"No, thank you, my dear." Emily's cheeks blushed attractively. "I won't intrude on your family time. Besides, I think I'm going to go to bed very early this evening."

Noreen eyed her neighbor closely, noting that despite the slight blush on her cheeks, she looked paler than usual. "Are you feeling all right?"

Emily smiled. "Just tired. I think it's this heat. It's far too early in the year for it to be so warm. I hope your father enjoys the pie."

"He'll love it." Noreen walked her neighbor to the door. "And you get some rest, okay?"

Noreen stood on the porch and watched Emily as she walked back to her house. Noreen had a sudden flash of herself in the distant future, living alone, cooking goodies for neighbors and fighting an ever-present loneliness. That's what her life would become if she didn't get past Jesse's betrayal, give her heart an opportunity to feel again.

Cindy had been right. It was time Noreen start dating again. But who? For nearly the past four years she'd rejected the overtures of most of the eligible bachelors in town.

Instantly a vision of Vinnie danced in her head. She shook her head and headed back to the kitchen. It was one thing to decide to place a toe in the frying pan, but dating Vinnie would be like plunging right into the fire.

Smoke. It clogged the air. Thick and black. Acrid and hot. Vinnie's lungs filled with it, burning…choking. He had to get up…do something to make the smoke stop. The heat that surrounded him threatened to blister his skin. He had to get up. He had to!

He knew it was a dream, the same one that had

haunted him for months immediately after the accident. He also knew no matter how he struggled, no matter how he fought against it, the dream would play to its usual, heart-ripping end.

Through the dark cloud of smoke, he saw the faint red glow of emergency vehicle lights flashing outside the house. *Help,* his mind screamed. Help my family.

He reached for Valerie, but she wasn't next to him. Then he remembered. He was on the sofa. She was upstairs in their bed. Help them, he cried as soot-filled tears burned his cheeks. For God's sake, somebody help them, please.

"Daddy."

The childish cry tore at him as he fought against the swirling darkness of unconsciousness. He needed to help. He needed to get up and save them. But he couldn't...couldn't breathe...couldn't move. God help him, he couldn't save them.

Consciousness came with the same startling abruptness as it had on that night so long ago. The only difference was that instead of finding himself in the front yard, being attended to by EMTs, he sat up in the bed and stared around the room in confusion.

No smoke. No flames. Just a small, second-floor rented apartment in Ridgeview, Kansas. He pulled himself out of bed, aware of the sheen of sweat that coated his body.

He unlocked the sliding door that led to a small balcony and stepped outside. The cool night air soothed both his body and spirit.

Raking a hand through his hair, he wondered what had brought the dream back. It had been months since he'd suffered that particular one. He'd thought they were finally gone for good.

He leaned against the balcony railing, noting the position of the moon. It must be around two o'clock. The house beneath him was silent. The Chatam family all slept soundly in their beds, undisturbed by nightmares of fire and death. He envied them that.

Mr. and Mrs. Chatam were a nice older couple, renting out the second story of their home to subsidize their social security income. The house was smack-dab in the center of Main Street, between the post office and the grocery store. The two-room apartment was perfect for a bachelor, and Vinnie was pleased with the accommodation.

He frowned, still fighting a disturbing unease at the recurrence of the nightmare. Lately he'd been missing the neat and orderly world he'd left behind, the paperwork and mental challenge of his law practice. Perhaps the dream had been sent to him to remind him of his commitment to fire fighting.

As a car approached, the high beams piercing the darkness of night, Vinnie stepped back into his room. It wouldn't be proper for somebody to see the newest member of the Ridgeview Fire Department standing on the balcony in his briefs.

He got back into bed, knowing from past experience the nightmare wouldn't return for the remainder of the night. Still, sleep remained elusive.

Coming to Ridgeview had been a good thing. He'd needed to get away from Chicago and the memories that haunted him. He folded his arms beneath his head and stared at the ceiling, his mind filling with a vision of Noreen.

She intrigued him more than any woman he'd met in the past year. Her quick wit amused him, made him laugh. It had felt good. God knew, there had been little genuine laughter in his life lately.

Vinnie loved women. He loved the scent of their perfume, the sound of their laughter. He'd missed having a companion in his life, a woman to share good times and a few laughs. The last thing he wanted was any kind of a commitment. He wasn't looking for a soul mate or a heart connection. He just wanted a good time.

Noreen didn't date, which implied she wasn't exactly actively seeking Prince Charming and a happily-ever-after commitment. As far as he was concerned, that made her perfect for him...at least for a while.

Chapter Four

"Mom, how do you get a baby?"

Noreen sank down on the sofa next to her son. They were waiting for Cindy and Jeffrey to pick them up for pizza. Yesterday Billy had wanted to know about his daddy, now today, how babies were made. "What's with you and babies?" she asked, buying time so she could figure out exactly how much or how little to tell him about procreation.

Billy shrugged. "I want one."

"What made you decide you want one?"

Billy's eyes lit with an earnest shine. "Larry Kline, he's in my class, and his mom had a baby a while ago. A girl baby. Larry's mom brought her to school last week and she was so little and so cute. Larry's her big brother, and I want to be a big brother, too."

Finally the mystery was solved, Noreen thought. She'd always believed that peer pressure would come in the form of wanting an expensive brand of tennis shoes or a football jacket. She'd never suspected her first taste of peer pressure from her son would be his desire for a baby in their life.

"Larry said his baby sister grew in his mom's tummy." Billy looked at her skeptically. "Is that true?"

"That's where babies grow until they are big enough to be born," Noreen explained. "You were in my tummy for nine whole months."

"I was?" He looked at her incredulously. "Wow. I thought Larry was just making that up." He stared at the book in his lap for a long moment, then looked back at Noreen. "Larry said the baby got in his mommy's stomach 'cause his mom and dad spent time alone together and his dad planted a seed."

She could tell by the way Billy looked at her that he wanted confirmation that Larry wasn't telling big white lies. She thought a moment, decided this particular story was close enough to the truth and not too much information for an almost-six-year-old to handle. "That's pretty much the way it happens," she replied.

She breathed a sigh of relief as a horn sounded from the driveway and Billy jumped up in excitement. "They're here. Come on, let's go." He dropped his book to the floor and grabbed Noreen's hand, all talk of baby and proliferation forgotten with the anticipation of spending time with his best friend.

Cousin Eddie's Pizza Palace was one of the most popular places in town. It wasn't just because Cousin Eddie's was the only place that served pizza, but rather because the restaurant not only catered to kids' tastes, but also to their entertainment.

A cavernous building housed arcade games, pinball machines and climbing equipment to please children of every age. The walls were lined with comfortable booths, where parents sat, ate and yelled at their children to stop playing and eat some pizza.

Noreen and Cindy found an empty booth and slid in, the boys already begging to be allowed to play the games. "Okay, go," Noreen said as she handed them each several dollars to exchange for tokens. "But when our pizza arrives, you two scamps better come back here to eat."

With hurried agreements, the two took off for their favorite game, where they battled each other as cyborg soldiers.

Cindy placed their usual order, then she and Noreen settled back in the booth for some serious gossip. "What a week," Cindy exclaimed. "The kids have been almost uncontrollable."

Noreen smiled. "You know they're always like that right before summer vacation. This afternoon, Mickey Brown got so excited talking about the trip his family is taking to Disneyland, he threw up."

Cindy laughed and shook her head. "Wish we were going to Disneyland. Looks like we're just going to be hanging around here for the summer, paying off credit cards."

"We'll keep you company. We aren't planning to go anywhere, either." Their conversation halted as the waitress appeared with their drink orders.

"So, no fun summer plans for you?" Cindy asked when the waitress departed.

Noreen shrugged. "Not really. I'm going to take Billy to day care two days a week and do some work around the house, paint inside and out."

"Sounds horrendous."

Again Noreen shrugged. "It needs to be done. It needed to be done four years ago. Jesse was always promising to get to it." For the first time, his name didn't invoke a wistful yearning or heartrending pain.

"Ah, yes, another in the long list of that creep's broken promises. The one good thing he ever did for you is leave."

Cindy, Jesse and Noreen had all gone to high school together, and Cindy had been one who had told Noreen over and over again not to marry him.

"He'll break your heart," she had warned Noreen. But Noreen, flush with passion and the glow of first love, had refused to believe her best friend.

"We have to find you a man," Cindy said decisively. "You've been hiding long enough. It's time to join life again."

"I haven't been hiding," Noreen protested. "And I have a life, thank you very much."

Cindy snorted. "Yeah, you fix dinner for your father almost every night and spend the rest of your time with second-graders and your son." She leaned forward. "You need a man. And some sex certainly wouldn't hurt."

"Cindy!" Noreen's face flamed with heat and she surreptitiously glanced around to make sure their conversation wasn't being overheard.

"Well, it's true. You're a young, attractive woman and you're allowing Jesse's betrayal to keep you alone."

"You win." Noreen threw up her hands, deciding a mock surrender was easier than arguing with her bullheaded friend. "Okay, I've decided to start dating, now there's just one problem. How do I begin?"

Cindy rubbed her hands together, then pulled a pad and pencil from her purse. "First we need to make a list of all the eligible bachelors in town, then we'll decide which ones we think are right for you."

"That sounds a bit cold and calculating, doesn't it?"

Cindy frowned at her. "Honey, the last time you made a decision about romance, you used your heart, not your head. Don't you think this time you'd be wiser to use your head?"

Noreen didn't reply, knowing her friend was probably right. Her decision to get involved with Jesse had led to a dismal failure. She didn't want to go through that kind of heartache again.

Maybe the best thing would be to marry a man she didn't love as helplessly, as overwhelmingly as she had Jesse. Maybe this time the smart thing would be to choose a man who would be responsible and committed. A man who would make a great father for Billy and a friendly companion for Noreen. Head, not hormones...yes, that was the safe way to pick a prospective mate.

"Okay, how about Martin Winthrop?" Cindy asked, pen poised on notepad.

Noreen shook her head. "He's off the market...back with his ex."

"Bobby Sanford?"

Noreen frowned. "I just can't consider dating a man who wears plaid socks."

"Walt Burgess?"

"Do you think that's really his own hair or a really bad toupee?"

Cindy dropped the pen and eyed Noreen with undisguised aggravation. "You aren't taking this seriously. You aren't even trying."

"I am," Noreen laughingly protested. "I just can't think of anyone here in Ridgeview that does anything for me." Her mind instantly conjured up a vision of dark, sexy eyes and a sensual smile that promised sinful indulgences.

"What about that sexy fireman who came to the school yesterday?" Cindy asked as if reading her mind.

"Out of the question," Noreen replied without any hesitation. She took another sip of her soda. "Actually, I had coffee with Vinnie yesterday after school," she confessed.

"You little sneak," Cindy exclaimed. "I knew there was something going on between the two of you. Every time you looked at each other sparks snapped in the air."

Noreen opened her mouth to protest, but closed it just as quickly, unable to deny the existence of those sparks. From the moment she'd first met Vinnie Pastorelli, she'd felt the arc of energy, a scintillating sexual excitement, flow between them.

"Sparks might have snapped, but I don't intend to do anything to fan those sparks into flames," Noreen finally said.

"Why not? The man is the right age, has a good job, and he's a total hunk. You'd be crazy not to fan those sparks."

Noreen took another sip of her drink, then sighed. "He shares too many characteristics with Jesse."

"Like what?"

"Like he's a natural flirt."

"But, Noreen, being a flirt doesn't mean being a cheat. Jesse was a rat fink, but that doesn't mean Vinnie is the same kind of man."

"I'm just not willing to find out," Noreen replied. She couldn't take a chance on being pulled into his charm and refused to allow her heart to be vulnerable to Vinnie's charisma.

She sighed in relief as their pizza arrived, effectively putting a halt to the subject of Noreen's love life, or lack of one. She and Cindy signaled the boys, who returned to the booth to eat.

The women insisted the boys slide into the booth and sit between the wall and their mothers, knowing the best way to see they ate was to trap them in the booth where they couldn't easily escape back to the games.

The pizza was accompanied with talk of space aliens and bugs, and all the things little boys found fascinating. As Noreen enjoyed her pizza, she gazed at her son lovingly. He was such a good boy and in those months after Jesse's desertion, after Noreen's mother's death, it had been Billy who'd kept her sane.

His laughter, his sloppy kisses and loving hugs had been the glue that had managed to piece her heart back together into some semblance of normalcy again.

She would love to give Billy a baby brother or sister. He'd make a loving, wonderful big brother. But more important, she wanted to give him a father, a man to look up to, a man to guide him through the growing-up process with love and discipline.

She leaned over and picked a strand of stringy cheese from her son's chin. He grinned, his mouth ringed with tomato sauce. "You have more pizza on you than in you," she observed.

He licked his lips. "I love pizza."

"Me, too," Jeffrey echoed.

"Is this a private party, or can anybody join?"

The deep masculine voice caused an unwelcomed swirl of heat to suffuse Noreen. She turned to see Vinnie standing just behind their booth.

"There's no such thing as private parties in Cousin Eddie's," Cindy replied. "Please join us," she gestured to the spot next to Noreen.

Noreen moved closer to her son, shooting daggers at her friend, who smiled innocuously.

Vinnie slid in next to Noreen, his closeness in the small confines both an irritant and a thrill. The scent of his evocative cologne teased her senses, and the press of his jeans-clad thigh against hers increased her internal temperature.

What was he doing here, she wondered peevishly. Cousin Eddie's wasn't exactly the local hangout for bachelor types. He focused his big brown eyes on

Noreen, eyes filled with humor and that breathtaking promise of something both wonderful and frightening. "You going to introduce me to your friend?" he asked.

"I'm Cindy, one of the teachers at the grade school. I know you're Vinnie the firefighter," Cindy said. "And this is my son, Jeffrey."

"I saw you yesterday at school," Jeffrey said. "You're going to give Billy's mom a baby."

Billy nodded. Cindy snorted with laughter. Vinnie grinned and Noreen's face flamed. "That particular rumor seems to be spreading," Vinnie said.

"Only among those too young to know better," Noreen replied.

"So, what brings you to Cousin Eddie's?" Cindy asked, her features retaining amusement as she looked from Vinnie to Noreen, then back to Vinnie again.

"I had a sudden craving for pizza," he answered. "And since this seems to be the only pizza place in town, here I am."

"Too bad we're just getting ready to leave, otherwise we could have kept you company while you eat," Noreen said, giving Cindy a pointed glare.

"Yeah, I guess we'd better get out of here if I'm going to let these two guys watch a video before bedtime. Billy is spending the night with Jeffrey," she explained to Vinnie. "And I still have to take Noreen all the way home." Cindy released a long-suffering sigh.

"I can take her home," Vinnie offered.

"Oh, that's not necessary," Noreen hurriedly protested.

"I really don't mind."

"Great," Cindy exclaimed. "Come on, boys, let's go home and watch those cartoon turtles you both love."

Before Noreen could lodge another protest, Cindy and the boys were up and heading for the door. Billy turned around and ran back to his mom.

"I forgot to kiss you goodbye," he said as he wrapped his arms around her neck. Noreen hugged his sturdy little body close, glad that he wasn't old enough yet to spurn kisses and hugs.

"Bye, honey. I'll pick you up in the morning at Cindy's," Noreen said.

Billy released his hold on her and shot a shy glance at Vinnie. "He's going to take you back to our house?" he asked in a pseudo whisper. "If you guys spend time alone, maybe you could work on the baby," he said, then turned and ran to rejoin Cindy and Jeffrey, who waited for him at the door.

She looked at Vinnie, who had shifted positions to now sit across from her. He grinned. "Your son seems to be fixated on a baby."

"Yes, one of his friends' mother had one recently, and Billy has decided he wants to be a big brother. And so far he isn't accepting no as an answer."

"Cindy seems nice. She a good friend?" he asked.

"She was," Noreen replied dryly.

Vinnie grinned. "Ah, go easy on her. This town seems to have a heavy percentage of matchmakers. One of the guys at the station has been trying to set me up with every eligible woman in town, although he tells me I'd be wise to steer clear of you."

Noreen looked at him in surprise. "Why?"

"He seems to think I'd be jeopardizing my relationship with the chief by dating you."

"Well, you don't have to worry about that because I don't intend to date you," Noreen retorted. "Shouldn't you signal the waitress about ordering?" she asked, still irritated by Cindy's manipulation.

He leaned forward and grinned. "I have a small confession to make. I hate pizza."

"Then why are you here?" she asked.

"You told me yesterday that you had a date with your son for pizza. Since this is the only pizza place in town, I thought I might find you here."

"Vinnie...I told you yesterday I don't date, and even if I did, I wouldn't date you."

"If you don't date, then what do you do for fun?"

"Contrary to most male beliefs, women can have fun without men."

He studied her closely. "Noreen, I'm not looking for a lifetime commitment here, but I like you. I'm new in town and could use a friend."

"I'm sure you don't lack companionship. You're attractive and charming and have an exceptional gift for blarney, you'll have no problems making 'friends.'"

He leaned back and eyed her with an expression of frustration. "You're a hard case, Noreen Simmons." He grinned again. "Lucky for you I don't give up easy—that I love challenges."

So had Jesse. He'd loved the challenge of the chase, but when he'd caught his quarry, he looked around for another challenge. "If you aren't going to order anything to eat, could you take me home now?'' she asked. Vinnie's pronouncement that he wasn't looking for any lifelong commitment only reinforced her knowledge that he was wrong...all wrong for her.

"Sure."

They were silent as they wove their way through kids and games to the front door. Sweet-scented night air greeted them as they stepped outside.

"Smells like summer," Vinnie observed as he led her to his car in the parking lot.

"Yes, it does." A faint pall of distant grief swept over her as she drew in the scent of grass and dark earth, of flowers and warm concrete. She shook her head to dispel the old feelings, refusing to allow Jesse to control her emotions any longer, and knowing her mother wouldn't want Noreen to grieve her passing another moment.

"This is your car?" she asked as he stopped to unlock the passenger door.

"Yeah...why do you look so surprised?"

She eyed the older model dark blue four-door sedan. "I don't know, I was expecting a little red sports car or something equally flashy."

He placed a hand on the car, his touch appearing almost caressing. "We...I bought this car on a very special day." His expression was as if the memory brought him both incredible joy and excruciating pain.

He pulled his hand from the car and opened the door for her to slide in, the odd expression usurped by a flippant grin. "Eventually when I trade it in, I just might check into one of those flashy red sports cars.''

He closed her door, then walked around to get into the driver side. Noreen had a feeling there was a lot more to Vinnie than his easy charm and flirtatious ways, a depth of emotion he seemed disinclined to share with anyone.

Not that she cared. He'd made it clear that he was simply looking for a good time, not a commitment. And she refused to settle for anything less.

''So, you want to go directly home or do you want to show me all the hot nightspots in Ridgeview?'' he asked as he slid behind the steering wheel.

Noreen smiled. ''There are no hot nightspots in Ridgeview.''

''Then how do the singles find each other?''

''Through the abundance of matchmakers you mentioned earlier. Of course there's the Moonglow Tavern where some of the single people occasionally hang out on the weekends, but the jukebox almost never works and there's a pool tournament almost always taking place.''

''Doesn't sound conducive to romance,'' he observed as he started the car and headed toward Noreen's house.

''You don't need a specific place for romance,'' she countered. ''All you need is a star-filled night, or the music of a breeze whispering through trees—'' She broke off with a blush.

''Why, Noreen, you're a closet romantic.''

''Most women are,'' she replied. ''And it's easy to

be a romantic when there's no man in your life to remind you of reality.''

Silence filled the car as if Vinnie wasn't quite sure how to respond. Noreen looked out the window, trying to ignore the scent of him that mingled with the night air blowing from the vents.

She gazed at him covertly. What was it about him that made her feel so utterly alive? All her senses seemed piqued when he was near.

"He must have been some piece of work," Vinnie said as he pulled into her driveway and shut off the engine.

"Who?" She wondered if she'd missed part of the conversation while ruminating on his effect on her.

He unbuckled his seat belt and turned to look at her. "Your ex."

"What do you know about Jesse?" she asked, wondering if the small town grapevine had filled him in on Jesse's infidelities. By the time she'd finally faced the fact that Jesse was cheating on her, to her mortification, she'd realized everyone in town had already known. "I suppose you've been listening to gossip around town."

"No. Actually, I didn't even know his name until this very minute. I just figure he must have been a fool to let you get away." He leaned toward her, his eyes gleaming in the semi-darkness. "Now, how about you invite me in for a cup of coffee and tell me about this ignorant man who was so bad he put you off dating."

Noreen's first instinct was to tell him no, that she

didn't want him in her house, didn't want him invading her personal space.

"What are you so afraid of, Noreen?" he asked softly. "Afraid if I come inside you won't be able to control your lust for me?"

Noreen recognized the teasing tone in his voice and responded with a reluctant laugh. The man really was incorrigible. "Okay. Come on in. I promise I'll try my best to control my lust for the duration of a cup of coffee."

They got out of the car and Noreen unlocked the front door and stepped inside, intensely aware of Vinnie just behind her. "Of course, I didn't make any promises about containing my own lust."

His soft, velvet voice created a shiver that danced up her spine. Apprehension or anticipation, she didn't know which she felt.

She turned and looked at him, trying to maintain her composure. "I'll make the coffee," she said, and ran for the kitchen.

Chapter Five

Vinnie had no idea what he was doing. Here...with her. He'd had no intention of seeking her out, had planned to grab a beer at the Moonglow Tavern, then call it an early night.

He'd been on his way to the tavern when he'd found himself in Cousin Eddie's parking lot. He'd sat in the car for fifteen minutes, battling with himself, before finally surrendering and heading inside.

As she made the coffee in the kitchen, he wandered around the living room. Although clean, the room was cluttered with signs of living. Video games tumbled out of the bookshelves that lined one wall, as if an eager hand had picked through the games looking for a favorite.

Magazines spilled across the worn wooden coffee table, battling for space with a floral centerpiece. He picked up a bottle of nail polish sitting on a small table next to a recliner. Reading the bottle, he smiled. Passion Pink.

"Can I help with anything?" he asked.

"No. Just make yourself at home," her voice drifted back to him from the kitchen.

Home. Yes, it was obvious this was a home, not a house. It was a place of refuge, of safety, a place to belong.

Vinnie had once had a place where he belonged, a house that had breathed laughter, with love as its heartbeat. He felt a sudden, swift ache for all that had been lost, the sweet yearning to have it once again.

He shook his head to dispel the emotions. He'd learned it was best to travel light, to never depend on that which could be taken away.

"Here we are." Noreen entered the living room carrying a tray laden with cups, a carafe, sugar and cream. She placed the tray on the magazines on the coffee table, then looked around with an expression of chagrin. "Sorry for the mess. I wasn't expecting company."

"Don't apologize." He sat down on the sofa and took the cup of brew she offered him. "I was just thinking that the room had a nice lived-in look."

She laughed. "That's quite diplomatic." She poured herself coffee, then perched on the edge of the sofa, as if ready to bolt at any moment.

"You can relax," he teased. "I promise if I feel lust overtaking me, I'll warn you well in advance." The pink that colored her cheeks charmed him. In truth, so far there was very little he'd found not charming about her. "So, are you going to tell me about your ex-husband or do I have to rely on local gossip to hear about him?''

She frowned. A flash of pain flickered in her eyes. ''I've had a nice evening. I really don't want to ruin it by talking about him.''

He nodded, wishing he hadn't brought it up. He didn't like to see any distress in her eyes. He wanted them dancing with humor, sparkling with laughter. ''Most women find my job fascinating, but I guess growing up with the chief, it's old hat to you.''

She smiled. ''And I'll bet when you're talking to women about your work, you exaggerate disgracefully.''

''Shamelessly,'' he agreed.

She laughed, the musical sound warming Vinnie. ''Unfortunately you can't do that with me.'' Her laughter faded, and she looked at him seriously. ''You mentioned yesterday that you have three sisters. That must be nice. I always wanted a brother or a sister.''

''At times nice. At times torturous.'' He settled back against the sofa cushions, a smile curving his lips as he thought of his sisters and those growing-up years. Despite the teasing and tormenting he'd endured from his older siblings, the four had been close. Until tragedy intruded. Until he'd had to gain distance to maintain his sanity. ''We aren't as close now as we used to be,'' he finished.

''That's too bad. When my mom died four years ago, I really wished I had a sibling to help me deal with the grief, somebody who could help me deal with Dad's mourning as well as my own.''

''Sometimes grief is too deep to share with anyone,

no matter how close to you they are." The conversation had gotten too personal and decidedly uncomfortable. As he struggled to think of a safer topic, the doorbell rang.

"Who on earth could that be?" Noreen asked as she got up to answer.

She opened the door, and an attractive older woman stepped inside. "Oh, I'm sorry. I didn't realize you had a gentleman caller," she said.

"Trust me, he's no gentleman," Noreen replied wryly.

Vinnie laughed and walked over to the woman. "Hi, I'm Vinnie Pastorelli." He took her frail hand in his. "And you are?"

"Emily Winston, Noreen's neighbor." Her pale cheeks pinkened and her blue eyes sparkled youthfully.

Vinnie gave her hand a soft squeeze, then released it. "It's nice to meet you, Mrs. Winston. Would you care to join us for a cup of coffee?"

"Oh, my, no. Caffeine this late would keep me up all night. But thank you for the invitation." She smiled, then turned to Noreen. "I came by earlier but you weren't home. I made a batch of those oatmeal cookies Billy loves." She handed Noreen a tin container.

"Emily, you spoil us," Noreen chided, affection apparent.

Vinnie felt a swift longing to hear that kind of fondness in her voice when she spoke to him.

"Nonsense," Emily protested. "You're a good

neighbor and a good friend. Besides, who else am I going to bake for if not you and Billy?''

''Are you sure you won't stay and have something to drink?'' Noreen asked.

''No dear. It's past my bedtime as it is. You enjoy your gentleman friend.'' She smiled at Vinnie, then looked back at Noreen. ''And I do believe, contrary to what you said, that he has the heart of a gentleman.'' Murmuring a goodbye to both Vinnie and Noreen, she turned and left.

''What a wise, wonderful lady,'' Vinnie exclaimed.

Noreen laughed. ''You just like her because you somehow managed to charm her.'' They sat back down on the sofa and she opened the tin of cookies. ''Want one?'' she offered.

''Thanks.'' He took a cookie, and she did the same. ''Hey, these are great,'' he exclaimed, the cookie a burst of oatmeal and cinnamon in his mouth.

''I'll send some home with you. Emily always sends too many for just the two of us.'' She finished her cookie, placed the tin on the table, then picked up her cup once again, her features reflective. ''Emily is such a sweet lady. She seems to have so much love to give. I wish she had somebody special in her life.''

''She's a widow?'' Vinnie guessed.

Noreen nodded. ''Her husband died seven years ago, and apparently they'd never been able to have children. I think she's terribly lonely. I worry about her.''

Vinnie suddenly felt the need to escape...run. The gentle caring on Noreen's face and the tenderness he saw in her eyes were bewitching. Somehow they seeped beneath the defenses that had kept him safe for so long.

He wanted to keep things superficial, fun and definitely nonthreatening. He did not want to get emotionally involved with her on any level. He'd had that and lost it.

"I guess I'll take off. I've got to be at the station early in the morning." He stood, ignoring her look of surprise. "Thanks for the coffee."

"Just a minute. I'll wrap up some of these cookies for you." She took the tin and disappeared into the kitchen.

The panic that had momentarily gripped him eased. He was lonely, and he sensed a loneliness in Noreen. Surely he could assuage some of his loneliness with her without losing his heart or giving away what was left of his soul.

He was in control, as he had been for the past two years. He smiled at her as she came back into the living room, a foil-wrapped package in her hand. "You really didn't have to do this," he said as he took the package from her.

"You said you don't do much cooking. I don't mind sharing." They walked to the front door and both stepped outside into the warm sweet-scented night air. "Besides, there's nothing better than a midnight snack of cookies and milk."

He had a sudden image of her in a soft pink nightgown, sitting at the kitchen table sharing cookies and milk with her son. He leaned toward her, taking a strand of her hair between two fingers. Soft. Silky, just as he'd known it would be.

Her eyes widened at his touch, and her mouth parted slightly. He knew if he kissed her, she'd taste of heat and a touch of cinnamon. He moved his hand from her hair to the smooth skin of her jaw, heard the intake of her breath and felt the racing of his own heart.

He wanted to kiss her, wanted it more than anything. And she knew that's what he wanted. And she wanted it, too. He could tell by the way her eyes shone in anticipation, by the fact that she didn't step back, but rather seemed to lean toward him.

She looked so pretty, with the moonlight stroking the strands of her hair and painting her features with a silvery glow.

"I'd love to kiss you," he said softly, his hand cupping her face. "But this isn't an official date, and it wouldn't be appropriate." He dropped his hand and stepped away from her. "But when you finally agree to go out with me, on a date, that is, I intend to kiss you thoroughly and completely."

Without waiting for her reply, he turned and walked down the porch to his car. He didn't look back until he pulled away from the curb. She still stood on the porch, just where he had left her. His hand tingled from the contact with her skin. He wondered if her heart beat as rapidly as his still did.

He wanted her, and it had been a very long time since he'd wanted anyone. He wanted to kiss those sweet lips, feel her silky skin naked against his. He wanted to make love to her in the quiet hours of the night, in the heat of the midday sun.

It was a curious dichotomy. He wanted her in his

life, but not in his heart. He wanted to make love to her, but refused to consider loving her. He wanted physical closeness without the vulnerability of emotional intimacy. He turned into his driveway, wondering if what he wanted was possible.

That night, he suffered no nightmares. Rather he dreamed of Noreen. He dreamed of laughter and love-making and awakened confused and disturbed.

As he dressed for work the next morning, he wondered if perhaps he wouldn't be smarter to distance himself from Noreen. There were plenty of other single women in Ridgeview, attractive women who didn't touch him in the private space of his heart where he wanted to remain untouched.

Still, as he drove to the station, he realized he didn't want to date any other woman. He liked Noreen. He enjoyed her acerbic wit, the verbal sparring between them, and he liked the challenge she presented. As long as she understood his rule of no commitment, there was no reason why he shouldn't continue to pursue her.

The moment Vinnie walked into the station, he knew something was amiss. Several of the men sat at the counter drinking coffee, their conversation less raucous, more subdued than usual.

As he walked over to them, their conversation halted abruptly.

"Hey, guys, what's up?" Vinnie asked. He poured himself a cup of coffee and joined them at the counter.

Sam frowned at Vinnie. "You're in the doghouse," he exclaimed.

Vinnie took a sip of his brew, raising an eyebrow at Sam's words. "What are you talking about?"

"The chief said as soon as you came in to tell you he wanted to see you, and he was breathing fire."

"So, what did you do?" Jay Brady, one of the old-timers, asked.

Vinnie laughed. "Nothing. Whatever he's breathing fire about, it can't be over anything I've done." Vinnie took several gulps of the coffee, then stood once again. "Guess I'll go see what's up."

As Vinnie made his way to the chief's office, he tried to think of anything he might have done to get himself in trouble. The last thing he'd done officially before his days off had begun was talk to the kids at the school. He knew he'd done a good job. Surely a complaint hadn't been lodged.

The chief's office was in a small room off the garage that housed Big Red, the Ridgeview Department fire truck. The garage door was open, the truck readied for action at all times.

He knocked on the chief's door, a brusque bark of "Enter" his reply. As Vinnie stepped into the small confines of the office, the chief looked up from his paperwork, his eyes radiating undisguised irritation.

"Pastorelli, I've assigned you to wax duty today on Big Red," he said.

Vinnie frowned. Normally this particular task was taken care of once a week by a professional service of three young men who waxed and shined the lumbering vehicle. "Sir, I don't understand, I thought we contracted that work out."

"Today I want it done by you. Is that a problem?"

Vinnie eyed the older man curiously, wondering what bee he'd sat on. "No, sir, not a problem."

"Then get to it."

Vinnie started for the door, but paused and turned back as the chief called his name again. "Heard through the grapevine you've been spending a little time with my daughter. Find another girlfriend." He shuffled the papers before him, an obvious dismissal.

Vinnie left the office and went back to the garage, where the fire truck awaited him. Waxing the behemoth was a tedious, tiring chore, and it absolutely amazed him that he'd been assigned this particular task as punishment. For seeing Noreen. For spending time with her.

"Unbelievable," he muttered as he went to the cabinet and withdrew the necessary polish and soft towels. Punished like a kid having to write a sentence a hundred times on the blackboard. Punished like an errant teen having to rake the lawn for missing curfew. Unbelievable.

He began at the front of the truck, applying a small amount of the pastelike wax. Thank goodness the chief wasn't privy to his dreams. If the old man knew what he'd dreamed the night before about his daughter, Vinnie wouldn't be polishing Big Red, he'd be wearing tire tracks across his body.

Vinnie frowned, wondering if Noreen was worth the obvious hassle he was in for if he pursued her. The town was full of attractive women. Maybe he'd be wise to look in another direction for a female companion. He'd have to think about it.

He stepped back and stared at the large fire truck.

Unfortunately, he'd have plenty of time to think today. Think and wax.

"Come on, Billy. It's time to go." Noreen stood at the front door, waiting for her son to join her.

"I'm coming." He raced out of his bedroom, a hand held up in triumph. "I had to find my lucky rock."

He opened his palm to display the ordinary river rock that only in a little boy's imagination could possess elements of magic and luck. He pocketed the lucky talisman. "Now I know I'll win one of the games."

Noreen couldn't remember the last time she'd seen her son so excited. Last year he'd been too small to participate in many of the contests of skill and luck that were held throughout the day at the Firemen's Picnic. This year, he intended to take part in each and every contest.

As they got in the car and Noreen secured the casserole dish of baked beans on the floor in the back seat, Billy kept up a continuous chatter.

It was a perfect day for a picnic, warm but with a light breeze that kept it from becoming stifling. School had finished for the year the day before and the Firemen's Picnic seemed a perfect way to officially kick off summer vacation.

"It's going to be a fun day, isn't it, Mom!" Billy exclaimed as they headed toward Mayor Robert Witham's property at the edge of town.

"It's going to be great," she agreed.

"Did you get my fishing pole?"

She nodded. "It's in the trunk, along with the balls and bats and your baseball glove." She grinned at him. "I think we just about emptied your room into the trunk of the car."

He returned her smile with one of his own. "And I have on my fastest tennis shoes so if they have races, I'll win."

"The important thing is not to win, but to have fun."

Billy's grin widened. "But it's most fun if you win," he countered, making her laugh.

The picnic was traditionally held on several acres of ground alongside a sparkling lake. Although the mayor officially owned the property, many of the town's gatherings were held there since Ridgeview had no city park or community center.

When Noreen and Billy pulled up, cars already were lined in a row, and long aluminum tables, set beneath a large oak tree were ready to receive the food picnickers brought. Several barbecue grills were fired up, their smoky scent filling the air with a hint of hickory.

The moment their car came to a halt, Billy exploded out, running to join a group of kids playing an impromptu game of kick ball. Noreen headed for the tables, her casserole in hand.

As she walked by the row of parked cars, her gaze automatically sought Vinnie's. It wasn't there. She hadn't seen or heard from him since the night he'd taken her home from Cousin Eddie's. His absence had been surprisingly disappointing.

However, she'd had a busy week, with the end of

school activities and dinner with her dad every night. She hadn't missed Vinnie. Not one bit, she told herself as she made her way to the tables where several women stood visiting.

"Hi, Noreen," Sam Rogers's wife, Wendy, greeted her.

"Hi, Wendy, good to see you again." Noreen smiled at the pretty young woman. "Looks like number three is about to burst into the world at any moment," she observed as she eyed Wendy's bulging tummy.

Wendy laughed and rubbed her stomach gently. "My due date is next week."

"Girl or a boy?" Noreen asked as she set her bean casserole on the table.

"We told the doctor we didn't want to know. Since we already have one of each, this one is a bonus so it really doesn't matter." Wendy grinned at Noreen. "I understand your son has been actively seeking somebody to make a baby with you."

Noreen groaned. "So the word is out around town."

Wendy laughed. "Not around town. Vinnie told Sam that your son announced in school that Vinnie was going to give you a baby."

Noreen shook her head. "I can't seem to get it through Billy's head that making babies isn't as easy as he thinks it is."

Wendy touched her stomach once again. "Oh, I don't know. It seems pretty easy to me. At least Billy has good taste in prospective fathers."

"Hmm, if you like Vinnie's type," Noreen replied.

She was irritated to discover that in merely speaking his name, her pulse rate accelerated.

"What woman in her right mind wouldn't like his type?" Wendy countered.

Relief flooded Noreen as several more women joined them and the conversation turned to more mundane topics. As the others spoke of the weather, children and mates, Noreen found her rebellious thoughts once again on Vinnie.

She'd enjoyed spending time with him the night he'd brought her home from the pizza place. Even after he'd left, some of his energy seemed to have remained behind, along with his distinctive, attractive scent. That energy had lit the dark corners, as his scent had filled her head.

She'd wanted him to kiss her. As they'd stood on the porch and he'd touched her hair, her face, more than anything she'd wanted to taste his lips. And in the week since she'd seen him, she wondered what other woman might be tasting his lips. And the fact that she wondered irritated her.

"Hey, darlin' girl." Charlie walked up to Noreen and wrapped her in a bear hug, dispelling all thoughts of Vinnie from her mind. "How long you been here?" he asked as he released her.

"Just a few minutes. What about you?"

"I've been here for hours getting things set up."

"It's going to be a gorgeous day," Noreen said, leading her father away from the group of women and over to a cooler of canned soda and ice. She plucked a diet drink from the cooler and popped the tab. "Want one?"

Charlie shook his head. "I've still got a few things to do before everyone gets here." He pointed toward the parking area. "Isn't that Emily Winston?"

Noreen turned to see her neighbor getting out of her car. "Oh, I'm so glad she decided to come. I invited her, but wasn't sure she'd make it." Noreen waved as Emily Winston approached.

"I don't think I've ever seen her in a pair of slacks before," Charlie said.

Emily was clad in a pair of pink slacks with a matching floral blouse that emphasized the attractive shade of her silver hair. As she drew closer, Noreen thought she saw her father stand a little taller, and one of his big hands swept hurriedly through his hair.

"Emily." He greeted her with a curt nod.

"Charlie," she returned his greeting, a slight flush of color staining her cheeks.

"I'd better get back to work. Nice seeing you here," Charlie said, then turned and left the two alone.

"I'm so glad you could make it," Noreen said.

"I decided it was too pretty a day to stay cooped up inside," Emily said as she and Noreen walked to the food table. Emily set her pie down and turned to Noreen. "I suddenly realized I've been letting my last little heart attack scare keep me from living. I've been staying close to home, afraid of going out for fear I might die. Then I realized that I might as well be dead if I'm going to stop living, anyway."

Noreen gave the woman a quick hug. "Well, I'm glad you're here."

"Actually, dear, I have you to thank for my new attitude," Emily said.

Noreen looked at her quizzically. "Me?"

Emily nodded. "The other night when I stopped by and saw you with your young man friend, I realized you were finally getting on with your life despite your previous heartbreak. You aren't letting fear rule your life, and that gave me the courage to do the same." She squeezed Noreen's arm. "And for that, I thank you." Her gaze went over Noreen's shoulder. "Oh, there's your young man now."

Noreen turned to see Vinnie getting out of his car. She wanted to insist that he wasn't her "young man," that Emily shouldn't draw courage from Noreen because Noreen had none. But as Vinnie approached, his lips curved in one of his damnable sexy smiles, the words of protest refused to escape from Noreen's mouth.

"Ah, if it isn't the two most lovely women in all of Ridgeview," he said as he approached them.

"And if it isn't Ridgeview's answer to a silver-tongued devil," Noreen returned, hating the way her heart stepped up its rhythm at his appearance.

He laughed good-naturedly, then smiled at Emily. "She's cruel, Mrs. Winston. Cruel and heartless."

"Cruel and heartless, perhaps," Emily agreed, light dancing in her eyes. "But you do have a bit of a silver-tongued devil in you."

Vinnie leaned closer to Emily. "But tell the truth—it's part of my overwhelming charm, right?"

Emily laughed. "Definitely," she agreed.

"Looks like it's going to be a fun day," Vinnie observed as he gazed around the area.

"Everyone always has a good time at these gatherings," Noreen replied, trying to ignore how handsome he looked in his tight jeans and the navy T-shirt. Bright yellow lettering, Ridgeview Fire Department, stretched across his firm chest.

"Guess I'll go see what's going on," he said. He smiled at Emily, then at Noreen. "I'll see you lovely ladies later," he said, then walked away.

Noreen watched him go, oddly disappointed that he hadn't stuck around to talk with them a little longer. Maybe he wasn't interested in her anymore.

She tried to summon relief at this thought. After all, she didn't want to date him, knew he had the potential to break her heart. He possessed every quality she didn't want in a man.

"You like him, don't you?" Emily asked softly.

Noreen sighed helplessly. "I find him the most conceited, irritating, aggravating man I've ever met." She sighed again. "Yes. I like him." The confession didn't bring with it a burst of joy, but rather the resigned dread of knowing she had a penchant for choosing men who were utterly wrong for her. And as usual she was running true to form.

Chapter Six

In the hours of waxing and polishing Big Red, Vinnie had come to the conclusion that perhaps Noreen Simmons wasn't worth the baggage that came with her. Baggage in the form of one stubborn, cantankerous, overprotective father who happened to be Vinnie's boss.

Vinnie had spent the past week shoving thoughts of Noreen out of his head, refusing to allow visions of the tantalizing brunette to taunt him. He couldn't help that she'd somehow invaded his dreams, appearing several nights in dreams that tormented him and made him wake hungry for her in the mornings.

The moment he got out of his car at the picnic and saw her standing there, her hair glistening in the sunlight, desire rippled through him, surprising in its intensity. She looked so good, in a pair of tight navy shorts and a red and blue sleeveless blouse that tied at her slender waist.

He'd greeted her and her neighbor, then had moved on, uncomfortable with how much he wanted to linger, watch the sun play in Noreen's hair, see that sexy smile of hers light up her face.

Instead, he'd moved to join a couple of men who were firing up a number of grills. The talk was shop, what was happening at the station, the budget cuts that affected the firemen and the hope that summer didn't bring a rash of fires.

Still, as the picnic officially got underway and the afternoon wore on, Vinnie's gaze continuously sought out Noreen.

He didn't understand it. She wasn't the prettiest woman at the picnic, nor was she the only single woman there. But she was the only one who caused Vinnie's blood to pound a little faster, his heart to beat more rapidly.

Maybe it was a case of the forbidden fruit syndrome. The guys at the station had warned him away from Noreen, and he'd waxed and polished Big Red as punishment for spending time with her. Vinnie had always been a perverse cuss. Maybe all the negativity merely served to fuel his desire for her.

Vinnie filled his plate and joined Sam and his wife, Wendy, at a table. "Hmm, this all looks great," he said.

"Picnic food always tastes good," Sam replied.

"Food I don't have to cook always tastes the best," Wendy added with a laugh.

"Where are your other rug rats?" Vinnie asked.

Wendy pointed to a distant area where a baseball

game was taking place. "First baseman and third baseman."

Sam leaned over and rubbed his wife's pregnant stomach. "And referee," he added. Sam and Wendy shared a look of such love, such anticipation for the birth of their child, Vinnie felt an unexpected pang of grief well up inside him.

He remembered. Heaven help him, he remembered too well the wild expectation, the bright hopes and dreams that came with the birth of a child. He remembered rubbing lotion on Valerie's swollen stomach, feeling the butterfly flutters of life within.

For a brief moment he tasted the bitter flavor of grief as he thought of all he'd lost, all that had been cruelly stolen from him.

He was grateful when the conversation turned once again to life at the station and work. Several other men joined them and as the conversation continued, Vinnie looked across to the next table where Noreen and her father sat eating.

What was the story of her ex-husband? She'd intrigued him on the night he'd asked about him, and she'd instantly accused him of listening to idle gossip. Whatever had caused their breakup, it had apparently fueled the town's rumor mill. And made her wary of relationships. How else could he explain her reluctance to date?

He frowned and jerked his gaze away, irritated by how easily she captured his thoughts, filled his head. Instead, he focused on the meal and the conversation of his friends.

After he finished eating, Vinnie wandered over to

where several of the men were setting up contests and races for the kids. Billy stood off to one side, his lower lip drooping nearly to the ground.

Vinnie looked around for Noreen and saw she was busy helping some of the women clean up the tables and cover the remaining food.

"Hey, kid, what's up?" Vinnie asked as he approached the little boy.

"They're getting ready to have a three-legged race and I only got two legs." Billy's lower lip quivered ominously. "I even wore my fastest tennis shoes so I could win all the races."

"Billy, you get another leg by getting another person to run the race with you," Vinnie explained.

Billy looked up at him, his eyes the same childish, poignant blue as those that haunted Vinnie's dreams. "All the boys are running the race with their dads, and I don't have one."

"What about your grandfather?" Vinnie suggested.

Billy winced and leaned closer to Vinnie. "Don't tell Grandpa I said this, but he's kinda old to be running races." Billy looked back over to where several of the men and their sons were getting their legs tied together in preparation for the event.

Don't get involved, Vinnie told himself. This isn't your problem. But the ache of wistfulness on the boy's face silenced the voice inside Vinnie's head. "If you want, I could be sort of a stand-in dad," Vinnie suggested.

Billy's face lit with excitement. "You could?" His little hand reached for Vinnie's, warmth seeping up

Vinnie's arm and directly to his heart as Billy squeezed his hand. "Come on, let's go!"

Vinnie found himself propelled forward by Billy's enthusiasm. They joined the other participants, laughing as they stood side by side and their legs were tied together in two places with sturdy twine.

"This is going to be fun," Billy said, his eyes dancing with excitement.

"It's a good thing I wore my fastest tennis shoes, too," Vinnie said, mentally throwing himself into the fun of the race, into comradery with the little boy. "You know, there's a secret to running a three-legged race."

"What?" Billy gazed up at him, eyes half-adoring.

"If we try to run fast, we'll fall. If we don't work together, we'll fall."

Billy listened intently, the freckles on his nose reminding Vinnie of the ones that danced across his mother's shoulders.

He looked around at the growing crowd of spectators and spied Noreen standing beside Emily Winston along the sidelines.

"There's your mother," he said to Billy.

Billy waved to Noreen. "Hi, Mom," he yelled. "We're gonna win the race. We both got on our fastest tennis shoes."

Noreen waved back and laughed, indicating she'd heard Billy. Her smile warmed Vinnie, who was suddenly glad he'd decided to follow his impulse and run the race with the fatherless boy.

"Racers get ready," Michael Walters yelled, a starting flag raised above his head.

"Remember, don't run," Vinnie said softly as he placed a hand on Billy's shoulder. "Just walk quickly and start with the foot that's tied."

Billy nodded, his gaze focused intently on the finish line in the distance. Vinnie felt the tension in Billy's sturdy shoulder and marveled at how important a race could be to a kid.

"Get set," Michael shouted. Tension filled Vinnie.

"Go!" The starting flag swept to the ground.

Billy and Vinnie took off, Vinnie quickly adjusting the length of his strides to accommodate Billy's shorter steps. The crowd of spectators erupted in cheers and shouts of encouragement. Vinnie could hear Noreen's voice amid the mix, cheering them to victory.

Several of the father-and-son teams fell, laughter and groans filling the air. Billy grinned up at Vinnie, his face flushed with excitement and the promise of success as they neared the finish line. "We're gonna win," he exclaimed. "We're gonna win!"

They didn't win. They pitched across the finish line, a tangle of arms and legs as they fell to the ground in third place.

Billy was a bundle of giggles as, in an effort to stand up, they both ended up back on the ground.

Vinnie's own laughter bubbled up as he tried to rise, stymied by the twine that tied them together. "Wait," he exclaimed as Billy tried again to get up. Billy's giggles were contagious as he fell atop Vinnie.

Still laughing, Vinnie untied their connection, then stood up and helped Billy up.

Billy threw his arms around Vinnie's neck. "We did okay," he said.

Vinnie laughed and picked him up. "Yeah, we did okay, but we didn't win."

"Oh, well," Billy replied easily. "We had fun." He placed a hand on Vinnie's cheek. His blue eyes peered into Vinnie's with the youthful truth of innocence. "You make a good dad."

Pain shimmered through Vinnie at the innocent words. Pain so intense it momentarily stole his breath away. He nodded curtly and set Billy down.

As Billy ran toward his mom, Vinnie turned and walked away from the crowd, needing some space, a moment of time to himself. He had to get himself under control, had to fight the pall of grief that threatened to suffocate him.

He headed for the pond in the distance, wanting to sort out the emotions that tore at his soul. "You make a good dad." Billy's words reverberated in Vinnie's head, echoing in the hollow chambers of his heart. And the little boy didn't know, couldn't know how wrong he was.

Fathers protected their children and kept them from harm. Fathers were there when their children needed them, to ward off bad dreams, to draw a circle of safety around them. Fathers didn't let their loved ones die.

For a brief moment, as Vinnie had held on to Billy, smelled the little-boy scent of unbridled excitement, of unexplored possibilities, for just a moment Vinnie had forgotten his loss.

Now the pain of that loss slammed into his chest

and tears burned behind his eyelids as he stared at the sparkling pond. An unexpected sob exploded from him and he clenched his fists, fighting for control.

"I knew there was some heartache beneath that charming smile."

Vinnie whirled around to see Emily Winston sitting beneath the shade of a tree near the edge of the pond. He hurriedly rubbed his eyes, irritated that she'd seen him in what he'd assumed was his private vulnerability. "I didn't see you there," he replied, his tone crisp and sharp.

"I know." She patted the ground beside her. "Come, sit with an old woman for a moment."

Vinnie walked over and sat in the cool, lush grass, still a bit embarrassed that she'd witnessed his momentary lapse of control over his emotions. He rarely went there, deep inside himself where his pain resided.

She was silent for a long moment, as if allowing him time to retrieve his dignity. "It's beautiful here, isn't it?" she finally said. "My husband, Ed, and I often came here to fish and talk." She smiled. "He'd fish. I'd talk. I'd pack a picnic lunch, and we'd spend the whole day here, just enjoying being together."

"How long has he been gone?" Vinnie asked.

"Seven years."

"Does the pain ever go away?" The question seeped softly from him with an aching need to know.

"Not entirely, but it becomes manageable, and eventually you realize you can't live in the grays of grief forever." She patted his hand. "I don't know what caused the grief you're clinging to, and it's really none of my business. But you need to remember that the soul couldn't have any rainbows if the eyes didn't have any tears.'' She gave his hand a final pat, then stood. ''And now this old woman is going to head home.''

''But the fun isn't over yet,'' Vinnie said, also rising to his feet.

''It is for me. I just came to please Noreen and Billy and say hello to that irascible father of hers.''

She tilted her head and gazed at him speculatively. ''She's a good woman, who has been wallowing in those grays of grief too long. The man who's bold enough to get past that bear of a father of hers won't be sorry he expended the effort.'' She gave him a little wave, then began walking toward where the cars were parked.

Vinnie stared after her for a long moment, then turned around and once again gazed at the pond. He was grateful she'd been there. Her presence had effectively stymied his descent into utter despair. He rarely allowed himself to dwell on his loss and the aching guilt that always accompanied such thoughts.

The past. It was all in the past. His life was here now, in Ridgeview. Alone. It was safest that way. Alone but not lonely. Vinnie Pastorelli, the flirting fool. He would fill his days and nights with fun, keeping those dark thoughts of the past at bay.

Noreen looked around the crowd, wondering where Vinnie had disappeared to. He'd vanished immediately after racing with Billy.

The games were in full swing, all the kids involved

in contests of skill and luck and supervised by several of the firefighters. She smiled as she saw Billy, helping set up bright orange highway cones for an obstacle course.

His red hair gleamed like a new penny, and the third-place medal he'd won in the three-legged race swung from a ribbon around his neck. The matching medal that should have gone to Vinnie was in Noreen's back pocket.

Where had Vinnie gone? Once again she scanned the crowd, then looked across the entire area, spying him in the distance by the pond.

Checking to make sure Billy was occupied, Noreen headed toward Vinnie, wanting to give him the medal and thank him for running the race with her son.

She'd been oddly disappointed that, for the duration of the day so far, he'd kept his distance from her. He'd come on so strong all the previous times she'd seen him.

When she'd dressed that morning she'd anticipated seeing him, verbally sparring with him, watching his sexy eyes make promises she didn't intend to allow him to act on. With this thought in mind, she'd added an extra touch of mascara and a dab of lipstick to her minimal makeup routine.

She'd been adamant that she didn't want to pursue any kind of a relationship with him, so why should she be disappointed that he'd apparently moved on?

She approached him from the back, trying to ignore the appealing width of his shoulders, the breadth of his back. His jeans hugged his slender waist, clung to his slim hips and butt. Definitely a cute butt.

A stick snapped beneath her feet, and Vinnie whirled around, his lips forming a smile. "Ah, the winsome Noreen. I was just thinking about you."

"You were?" Nerves fluttered in her stomach. Drat the man, he always seemed to do or say something to keep her off balance.

She dug into her back pocket and withdrew the medal. "I brought you this. You disappeared before you could get it." She handed him the medal. "And I wanted to thank you for running the race with Billy. You're not only one of his favorite firefighters, but now you've become his hero."

To her surprise, a faint blush stole over his features. "I don't want to be anyone's hero," he scoffed. "The kid needed a partner and I just happened to be standing there." He touched her arm, the light touch sending electricity through her veins. "Come and take a walk with me," he said.

She nodded, unsure why she agreed. There was absolutely no point in spending time with him, no reason for her to seek his company in any way. But she didn't even consider walking away.

They strolled around the edge of the pond, the cheers and noise from the picnic area growing more distant with each step.

"It's nice out here, isn't it?" he said.

"Yes, beautiful." She smiled shyly. "My ex-husband and I used to park here when we were dating. I think this place is still used as a Lovers Lane by the teenagers." Funny, as she thought of Jesse, there was no pain, no lingering ache. She felt only a sadness that she'd been a fool where he was concerned and a strange pity for him because she knew Jesse would probably forever be incapable of real love.

"You ever going to tell me about your ex or are you going to make me rely on gossip?"

She looked at Vinnie, noting how the sun stroked the rich darkness of his hair, how his eyes radiated with warmth to rival the sun's kiss on her shoulders and back. "Why do you want to know about him?"

He shrugged. "Curiosity. I figure if we're going to get more involved, I should know about your past."

"But I've told you, we aren't going to get involved," she returned, enjoying the teasing sparkle in his eyes. "Besides," she relented, not wanting to make Jesse into some sort of big mystery. "There really isn't that much to tell. I married Jesse because I loved him and I thought he loved me. He did love me...he just didn't let our marriage stop him from loving other women as well."

"Ah, a regular Don Juan."

She shook her head ruefully. "Sometimes I think Jesse left me, left Ridgeview, only because he'd managed to bed all the available women in town and needed new territory."

"That must have been tough."

"Yes, but even tougher was that somehow I embraced all the fault as my own. I should have tried harder to make him happy. If only I'd been more loving, or hadn't gotten pregnant so quickly, or hadn't gained so much weight with my pregnancy...the pregnancy really turned him off." She broke off, embarrassed to discover she'd said more than she'd intended.

Vinnie stopped walking and turned to face her. "I can't imagine anything more beautiful than a woman pregnant with my child." His voice shook with the strength of emotion. He leaned down and picked up a rock, then tossed it at the water. "Your husband was a fool. He threw away what should be cherished and protected."

Noreen looked at him curiously. "Not exactly the sentiments of an avowed bachelor," she observed softly.

He flashed her one of his bright smiles. "Don't let my occasional sentimental streak fool you. I intend to remain a bachelor for the rest of my life."

And that's exactly why she didn't intend to date him, Noreen thought. They continued to walk around the pond, the warm, late-afternoon sun tempered by a gentle breeze.

"You know, when you finally decide to date again, you're going to have a tough time of it with your guard dog," Vinnie said.

Noreen frowned at him curiously. "You mean Billy?"

"Your father. He's not too eager to share you."

Noreen laughed. "Dad just wants me to be happy." She leaned down and plucked a purple wildflower, then breathed in the sweet fragrance.

"Trust me," Vinnie said dryly. "He might want you to be happy, but he intends to keep potential suitors away from you. I've already felt the sting of his protectiveness where you are concerned."

She looked at him in surprise. "What do you mean?"

"Your father heard we'd spent time together, and the result was that I was assigned wax-and-polish duty on Big Red. Sort of like getting latrine duty in the army."

Noreen frowned thoughtfully and leaned against a tree trunk. "My mother died the same summer that Jesse left me." She gazed off into the distance. "That was a terrible summer for me and my father. We'd both lost our anchors, and I guess we decided if we held on to each other we wouldn't drown."

"Yeah, but that's been what, three...four years ago?" Vinnie asked.

"Four years."

"That's a long time to keep each other company to the exclusion of all others. Your dad is a vital man who might find a new companion, if he didn't have you to fill his lonely hours."

Noreen frowned again, thinking about it. Yes, her father was an energetic man who should have somebody special in his life. The thought of somebody replacing her mother didn't bother her, for she knew another woman in Charlie's life wouldn't be a replacement, but rather an addition.

"Don't you think maybe it's time you stopped holding on so tight to your father and start letting others into your life?" He placed a hand on either side of her, pinning her against the tree, although keeping his body a step away from her.

"You mean somebody like you?" Noreen's heart beat fast at his nearness. "Now why on earth would I want a confirmed bachelor who's an audacious flirt in my life?"

"For fun." He took one finger and traced the line of her jaw. Noreen fought against a shiver that tried to shimmy up her spine as his touch trailed sweet warmth. "Just for fun," he repeated. "Surely you aren't going to allow your experience with your ex-husband to make you forgo the pleasure of male companionship for the rest of your life?"

"No, it's just—" She broke off as his finger moved across her lips, making it impossible for her to think of anything but his touch.

He leaned closer to her, his wild, masculine scent enveloping her. "You remember the other night? When I told you I'd kiss you on our first date?"

She nodded, unable to find the breath to make a verbal reply. Even though she knew it was wrong—he was all wrong for her—she wanted to melt against him. She desperately wanted to run her hands up and down his strong biceps, feel the play of the muscles across his back.

"I've decided I don't want to wait for a date. I want to kiss you right now." With those words, he lowered his head and captured her lips with his.

Chapter Seven

Vinnie knew her mouth would be sweet, and it was...achingly sweet. What he hadn't expected was the heated hunger of her response. He'd intended a light, teasing kiss, but the moment she placed her hands on his shoulders, then wound them around his neck, light and teasing transformed to hot and hungry. Her open mouth invited him to explore, her tongue dancing with his in utter abandon.

She leaned into him, her breasts pressing against his chest, stirring a fever pitch of desire within him. He ran his hands down her back, finding the satiny warmth of the bare skin between the bottom of her blouse and the top of her shorts.

She moaned as Vinnie broke the kiss, his lips leaving hers to taste the sweetness of her neck, the fragrant length of her throat.

It had been years since Vinnie had felt anything remotely like the desire to make love. Although he'd enjoyed kisses, light caresses on dates with other women, he hadn't experienced this depth of desire with anyone else for a very long time. He wanted to make love to her. He wanted to lose himself in her warmth, discover himself in her heat.

He slid his hands up her back, beneath her blouse, loving the feel of her skin against his palms. Soft, so soft. He'd forgotten how warm and silky feminine skin could be. His palms reveled in the sensory delight of touching her, caressing her.

He felt the shiver that coursed through her as he kissed the smattering of freckles on her shoulders. He wanted her. His desire stole his breath away, making it difficult to breathe without gasping for air.

He knew she wanted him, too. He knew it by the way her hands clutched at his shoulders, the way her body molded intimately against his. He felt her hunger in the heated sighs she emitted against his neck.

Easing back from her slightly, he looked into her eyes.

"Noreen, there is nothing I'd like more than to sink down into this grass and make slow, sweet love to you." He touched her cheek and took another step backward, his gaze going to the crowd in the distance. "Unfortunately, now is not the time or the place."

The passionate glaze of her eyes cleared, replaced by cold reality and a touch of embarrassment. "What makes you think I'm the least bit interested in making love to you?" she asked, her husky voice betraying her attempt at studied indifference.

Vinnie smiled. "From the moment I met you, I felt

HOW TO PLAY:

1. Play the tic-tac-toe scratch-off game at the right for your FREE BOOKS and FREE GIFT!

2. Send back this card and you'll receive TWO brand-new Silhouette Romance® novels. These books have a cover price of $3.50 each, but they are yours to keep absolutely free.

3. There's no catch. You're under no obligation to buy anything. We charge nothing — ZERO — for your first shipment. And you don't have to make any minimum number of purchases — not even one!

4. The fact is, thousands of readers enjoy receiving books by mail from the Silhouette Reader Service™ months before they're available in stores. They like the convenience of home delivery, and they love our discount prices!

5. We hope that after receiving your free books you'll want to remain a subscriber. But the choice is yours — to continue or cancel, any time at all! So why not take us up on our invitation, with no risk of any kind. You'll be glad you did!

YOURS FREE
A FABULOUS MYSTERY GIFT!

**We can't tell you what it is...
but we're sure you'll like it!**

A FREE GIFT —
just for playing

TIC-TAC-TOE!

DETACH AND MAIL CARD TODAY!

First, scratch the gold boxes on the tic-tac-toe board. Then remove the "X" sticker from the front and affix it so that you get three X's in a row. This means you can get TWO FREE Silhouette Romance® novels and a **FREE MYSTERY GIFT!**

PLAY **TIC-TAC-TOE**

YES! Please send me all the gifts for which I qualify. I understand that I am under no obligation to purchase any books, as explained on the back of this card.

(U-SIL-R-08/98)

215 SDL CH6S

Name		
	(PLEASE PRINT CLEARLY)	
Address		Apt.#
City	State	Zip

The Silhouette Reader Service™ — Here's how it works:

Accepting free books places you under no obligation to buy anything. You may keep the books and gift and return the shipping statement marked "cancel." If you do not cancel, about a month later we'll send you 6 additional novels and bill you just $2.90 each, plus 25¢ delivery per book and applicable sales tax, if any.* That's the complete price — and compared to cover prices of $3.50 each — quite a bargain! You may cancel at any time, but if you choose to continue, every month we'll send you 6 more books, which you may either purchase at the discount price...or return to us and cancel your subscription.

*Terms and prices subject to change without notice. Sales tax applicable in N.Y.

If offer card is missing write to: Silhouette Reader Service, 3010 Walden Ave., P.O. Box 1867, Buffalo NY 14240-1867

BUSINESS REPLY MAIL
FIRST-CLASS MAIL   PERMIT NO. 717   BUFFALO, NY

POSTAGE WILL BE PAID BY ADDRESSEE

SILHOUETTE READER SERVICE
3010 WALDEN AVE
PO BOX 1867
BUFFALO NY 14240-9952

NO POSTAGE
NECESSARY
IF MAILED
IN THE
UNITED STATES

an electricity between us,'' he said truthfully. ''And you can't deny that you feel it, too.''

''Okay,'' she admitted, her cheeks stained a bewitching pink. ''You're right. I'm attracted to you, but that doesn't mean I intend to follow through on that attraction.''

''Why not?'' Vinnie asked as they started walking back around the pond.

''Because you aren't what I want in my life. Because despite the fact I find you physically attractive, I know you aren't right for me.''

''That doesn't mean we can't see each other, have fun together while you search for Mr. Right,'' Vinnie countered.

She arched an eyebrow at him, then laughed. ''At least you get an A for persistence.''

He grinned. ''You're going to discover I'm a very persistent kind of guy.''

She gestured toward the picnic area. ''We'll see just how persistent you are.''

Vinnie followed her gaze, spying the chief standing at the edge of the crowd, his disapproving scowl evident despite the distance. Vinnie's stomach knotted with anxiety. But when he looked at Noreen once again, the anxiety vanished.

The late-afternoon sun stroked touches of fire in her auburn hair, and her eyes rivaled the blue of the sky. As he thought of the kiss they'd shared, the hungry response of her lips against his, he smiled. ''If I have to wax and polish Big Red every day for the next month, kissing you was worth it.'' He fought the impulse to take her in his arms once more. "And what's more, I intend to kiss you again and again."

Her eyes widened, and her blush deepened. At that moment Billy ran toward them, halting the intimate nature of the conversation.

"Look, I got a trophy," he exclaimed, the plastic award held in both hands like a precious piece of sculpture. He beamed at both of them, his little chest puffed with pride. "I told you I had on my fastest tennis shoes," he said to Vinnie. "And I won the obsickle race."

"Obstacle," Noreen corrected him.

"Yeah, that." He looked from his mom to Vinnie. "So, were you guys off making my baby?"

Vinnie laughed. "Talk about persistence. I think I could learn something about that from Billy." Vinnie scooped the child up in his arms. "Come on, let's go see if we can find some marshmallows to roast."

Together the three of them walked back to where the games were breaking up and a large bonfire had been started to allow the kids to cook marshmallows.

Some of the people who didn't have children were starting to pack up and go home. Cars left, swirling dust behind them as the people who remained behind crowded around the fire.

Vinnie helped Billy skewer several of the fluffy sweets onto a prepared stick, then sat down at a nearby table next to Noreen.

Twilight approached, painting the sky in the west with soft lavenders and pinks. As Vinnie smelled the sweet fragrance of Noreen's perfume, watched the red-haired little boy burning marshmallows to a crisp, he felt a moment of peace.

This was the time of day when he often felt a vague sense of loneliness, when memories of what he'd once had, all that had been taken from him, returned to haunt him. But it was impossible to be haunted by specters from the past with Billy's giggles riding the air and Noreen's nearness filling his senses.

"Here you go, you guys can have the first two," Billy said as he held out two burned marshmallows barely clinging to the stick.

"No, thanks, Billy," Vinnie said. "I'm not much of a marshmallow eater."

"Well I am," Noreen exclaimed. They laughed as she pulled one of the sticky treats from the stick and popped it into her mouth. In the process she managed to decorate the side of her mouth with a glob of the gooey centers.

"What a mess," Billy said with a giggle, then took off to roast some more.

With a self-conscious laugh, Noreen used her finger and tongue to capture the bits of marshmallow. Desire once again soared through Vinnie. He envisioned himself leaning toward her, swirling his tongue across her lips, tasting the sweet concoction of marshmallow combined with the honeyed flavor of her mouth.

As if she could read his mind, Noreen's laughter died and her eyes flamed the indigo blue of desire. She leaned toward him, as if responding...no, eagerly participating in his fantasy.

"Pastorelli!"

The deep voice tried to penetrate the veil of desire

in Vinnie's head, but he ignored it, not wanting to shatter the sweet connection between himself and Noreen.

"Hey, Pastorelli! Come and help me with these."

Vinnie released an irritated sigh and looked over to where Sam was picking up the orange highway cones that had been used in the obstacle race.

"I'll be right back," Vinnie said to Noreen, who nodded and averted her gaze from his.

"What are you trying to do? Stay permanently in the doghouse?" Sam asked as he thrust an armload of cones at Vinnie.

"I don't know what you're talking about," Vinnie replied with mock innocence.

"Yes, you do." Sam scowled at him. "Of all the women in town, why do you have to have the hots for the chief's daughter?"

Vinnie laughed. "The hots? Men our age don't get the hots, Sam." He followed behind his friend as Sam continued picking up the rest of the cones.

"Then what in the heck are you doing with her? Courting trouble, that's what you're doing."

"She needs somebody to shake up her life," Vinnie said thoughtfully. He gazed over to where Noreen had joined Billy at the edge of the bonfire.

Four years. For four years she had shied away from dating, from relationships. If Vinnie could successfully pull her out of her defensive shell, if he could break the chains he suspected her father had wrapped around her when his wife died, then Vinnie would be happy.

"If you break her heart, the chief is gonna break your neck," Sam said softly.

Again Vinnie laughed. "I'm not out to break anyone's heart. Noreen knows where I'm coming from. She knows the last thing I want is any emotional entanglement or long-term commitment. I've been honest with her."

"So, what's your interest?" Sam paused and eyed Vinnie curiously.

Vinnie's gaze sought her out once more. The first response that leaped to his lips was that his interest was a result of hormones. Raw physical attraction. Spontaneous combustion.

But it was more than that. He liked the way she laughed, how a tiny wrinkle appeared across her forehead when she was deep in thought. He enjoyed watching her with her son, admired her firm yet affectionate parenting style.

"Earth to Vinnie."

Vinnie snapped his attention back to Sam. "What?"

Sam sighed in frustration. "Why in the heck are you pursuing this thing with Noreen when you know it's going to lead to nothing but trouble for you at work?"

Vinnie stared at his friend, searching his own mind for a rational answer. "I'm not sure," he finally admitted. "I just think she's had enough tears, and now it's time for a few rainbows."

Sam shook his head. "You're crazy, Pastorelli."

Vinnie grinned. "You're probably right," he agreed easily.

* * *

"Good morning." Emily greeted Noreen first thing the next morning. The older woman stood on Noreen's porch, a pie in hand.

"Are you already up and baking this morning?" Noreen asked in surprise.

"I promised the church ladies I'd have three pies ready for their spaghetti dinner this evening and decided to get an early start." She held it out to Noreen. "I had enough pastry left to make an extra one, and I know how your daddy is partial to cherry."

"Dad should be here anytime for a quick cup of coffee before work. Why don't you come inside?"

"Thanks, but I've got the other pies in the oven."

"You spoil us terribly," Noreen chided as she took the cherry pie.

"I like having somebody to spoil." Emily smiled, a sweet smile that brought youth dancing in her eyes. "Besides, your father works so hard keeping us all safe from fires here in Ridgeview, he deserves a little spoiling." Emily's cheeks pinkened slightly. "And now I'd better get back home." Saying goodbye, she walked across the lawns to her house.

Noreen watched her go, for the first time seeing her neighbor objectively. All the cakes and goodies she baked and brought over, and always a little something special for Charlie. Was it possible Emily was sweet on him?

Noreen carried the pie into the house and set it on the countertop, her mind whirling with possibilities for matchmaking. Why not?

Vinnie had been right the day before, when he'd said that she and her father were clinging to each other, refusing to allow others in. He'd simply mirrored the same things Cindy had been telling her for months, that it was time they learn not to cling so tightly to each other.

Emily and Charlie. She smiled at the thought. Both were lonely, both were about the same age, and Emily had many of the characteristics Noreen's mother had had.

The idea still whirled around in her head a few minutes later when she served her father coffee. "The picnic yesterday was a rousing success," Noreen said.

"It was nice, wasn't it?" Charlie leaned back in the chair, a self-satisfied smile on his face. "So, now that school is out and you're a lady of leisure, what are you going to do with your time?" he asked.

"Lady of leisure, indeed," Noreen scoffed. "Today I'm taking Billy to day care for the day, and I'm going to paint my bedroom."

"If you want to wait a couple of days, I'd be glad to help you on my time off," Charlie offered.

"Thanks, Dad, but I'm eager to get started." She took a sip of coffee, not telling him that she was looking forward to the physical exertion of the chore, hoping it would ease the craziness that had possessed her from the moment Vinnie had kissed her.

Craziness. There was no other way to describe the night of tossing and turning, burning and shivering, remembering and replaying. Utter madness.

"Dad, do you ever think of dating?"

Charlie looked at her as if she'd lost her mind. "Dating? Me?" He snorted. "Who would want to date an old codger like me?"

"I'm sure there are a lot of women who would find you attractive," Noreen countered.

Charlie snorted again. "Only if she's old enough to be blind. Besides, what would your mother think? She'd roll over in her grave."

"I think Mother would be happy if you found somebody to share your life with. Dad..." She reached over and covered his hand with hers. "She's been gone a long time. Jesse has been gone a long time, too. Isn't it time we both move on?"

Charlie jerked his hand from hers, a scowl deepening the wrinkles on his face. "What brought up all this nonsense? I like my life just fine as it is."

"You don't have a life, Dad," Noreen protested.

"I most certainly do. I have you and Billy, and that's all I need." He narrowed his eyes. "He's got you thinking all this nonsense, doesn't he?"

"Who?" Noreen asked, although she knew exactly who Charlie meant.

"Pastorelli." He spat the name as if it tasted bad. "That man is trouble. He's filling your head with foolishness, and he doesn't have a sincere bone in his body." Charlie gulped the last of his coffee and stood. "I'm telling you, doll, don't get mixed up with him. He'll break your heart."

Noreen stood and gave her dad a hug. "Don't you worry about my heart. It's safe and sound, and I intend to keep it that way."

Charlie patted her back, then released her. "I've got to get to work. See you tonight?"

She nodded. "Meat loaf."

"Sounds good. See you about six."

It wasn't until nearly an hour later, as Noreen drove home from taking Billy to day care that she found herself replaying once again the kiss she'd shared with Vinnie.

She should have known he'd be a master at kissing. He probably practiced a lot. But oh, how that man could kiss. His mouth had been an invitation to sin, offering delicious sensations that could make a woman forget everything else.

The death of her marriage had also brought an end to physical, sexual pleasure. Kissing Vinnie had made Noreen remember that she was a healthy, normal young woman who'd always enjoyed lovemaking. Vinnie had reawakened a part of her she'd thought Jesse had taken with him when he'd left.

There was a part of her that was pleased with the awakening, happy to discover that Jesse hadn't managed to somehow steal that part of her. However, there was another portion of her that wondered, now that she'd been awakened, what happened now?

She couldn't deny that she was vastly attracted to Vinnie, but she wasn't interested in a physical relationship without emotional commitment. And Vinnie had made it clear he wasn't interested in anything but a fun, noncommitted sexual fling.

As she pulled into her driveway, she frowned, wondering why there were times she was certain she saw shadows in Vinnie's eyes. Dark shadows that whispered of pain, of loss, shadows that spoke of a depth belied by his easy charm.

Shoving thoughts of Vinnie from her head, she got out of her car and headed back inside.

Despite the heat already building, portending an unusually warm June day, Noreen shut off the air-conditioning and went around the house opening windows. If she was going to paint, she'd want the ventilation.

After changing into an old pair of shorts and a cropped T-shirt that had been cut too short and exposed too much skin to wear in public, she opened a can of paint and started the process of transforming the walls.

She'd spent the early morning covering the bedroom furniture with old sheets and drop cloths. After Jesse had left, she'd wanted to change the room, as if by painting and buying new furniture she could make painful memories go away. But at that time she'd had neither the money nor the energy to make the changes.

Now she realized she no longer had the frantic need to paint away memories of Jesse. The memories were a part of her, just like the freckles on her shoulders and the hue of her hair.

Just as Vinnie had awakened her sexually, she was also on the verge of an emotional awakening. Her marriage to Jesse, the memories both good and bad, were firmly in the past, and for the first time she looked forward to a future…a future spent not alone, but with a special man.

A vision of Vinnie filled her head—Vinnie, his leg tied to her son's and laughing as they crossed the finish line. Vinnie, eyes glowing with desire as he touched her face, her hair. Vinnie…exciting, stimulating, and definitely not right for her.

Shoving thoughts of Vinnie from her head, she filled a brush with paint and crawled up the ladder in one corner of her room. She'd paint the area around the ceiling and baseboards first, then roll on the rest of it.

She'd chosen a buttercup yellow that would match the curtains and bedspread and give the room a cheerful aura of sunshine. She worked mindlessly, humming beneath her breath, pleased as the walls changed from dirty white to sunny yellow.

Time slipped away as she worked. The heat in the house climbed as the morning passed into early afternoon. She stopped occasionally to lift her hair off her neck and pluck her damp T-shirt away from her skin. She was taking one of those quick breaks when the doorbell rang.

As she climbed down the ladder, she felt a little woozy.

She clung to the rungs for a moment, taking deep breaths until the dizziness passed. Hurrying to the door, she tried to ignore the headache that banged at the base of her skull.

She opened the front door. "Vinnie!" She stared at him in surprise. "What are you doing here?"

He smiled. "I thought I'd drop in and see if I could take you to lunch, but it's obvious I can't because you're speckled."

"Speckled?"

He stepped inside and touched the tip of her nose. "You have speckles all over you...yellow speckles." He frowned as she leaned against the door, once again fighting a slight edge of dizziness. "It smells like a paint factory in here."

"I'm painting my bedroom."

"You all right?"

She nodded and released her hold on the door. "I'm just a little bit dizzy...probably all this heat."

He took her hand and led her to the sofa, motioning her to sit, then he took off down the hallway toward her bedroom.

"Vinnie!" She hurried after him, oddly disturbed by the thought of him in her bedroom. He'd already been there, in her dreams, but she wasn't sure she wanted him there in reality, filling her personal space with his scent, his energy, his presence.

"It's no wonder you're dizzy," Vinnie exclaimed as he stood at the foot of her bed in the center of her room. "It's so hot in here, and the fumes are so thick it's a wonder you didn't pass out altogether."

"But I've got the windows open," Noreen exclaimed.

"And there's not a breath of air moving today. It's so still and humid the fumes are staying right here. You have a fan?"

"There's an old box fan in the basement," she said.

"Point me to the basement, and I'll go get it."

She frowned, trying to remember exactly where she'd last seen the fan. "In the kitchen, the door next to the pantry goes to the basement. The fan is in the corner by the furnace."

The moment he left the room, her first impulse was

to run to the mirror, scrub off the paint that splattered her face, then jump into makeup and clean clothes.

Instead she sank down on the edge of the bed, too exhausted to care that she looked horrible. Besides, what did it matter? She wasn't trying to impress Vinnie Pastorelli.

"Here we go," he said as he reentered the room, large box fan in tow. He set the fan near the doorway and turned it on, the air instantly shooting toward the window and creating a refreshing breeze on Noreen's heated skin. "Stay right there and cool off," he commanded. "I'll be right back." Once again he left the room.

He returned a moment later carrying two tall glasses of iced tea. He handed her one, then sat down next to her on the bed. "Feeling better?" he asked.

She nodded and took several long gulps of the tea. "I didn't realize how thirsty I was," she said.

"With this heat and humidity, it's easy to get dehydrated." He leaned back on his elbows, looking obscenely attractive against the pale pink sheet. "Nice color," he observed, looking at the walls where she'd been working. His gaze lingered on her, making her overly conscious of the brevity of her T-shirt, the shortness of her shorts. "Comfortable bed," he said, his voice deep and slightly husky.

Noreen stood, refusing to be pulled into doing something stupid by the seduction in his eyes. "You said something about lunch. I don't want to go out, but as long as you don't expect anything more gourmet than sandwiches, you can eat here with me."

He grinned at her, as if knowing his enticing power

over her, as if he understood her need to run to a less-threatening room of the house. He got up and followed her to the kitchen.

"Make yourself at home." She gestured to the table. "I'll be right back, I just need to clean up a little bit."

In the bathroom, Noreen scrubbed her face with a washcloth to remove the paint splatters. She thought about changing clothes, then rejected the idea, refusing to allow his hot gazes or teasing smiles to make her uncomfortable.

When she returned to the kitchen, he was standing at the window, staring out into the backyard. He turned as she entered the room. "I see Billy has a tent set up out back."

Noreen nodded. "Dad got it for him a week ago." She went to the refrigerator and pulled out leftover ham, a tomato and a head of lettuce as Vinnie sat down at the table. "Billy has been practicing camping out during the days. He wants me to take him on a camping trip sometime later this summer." She frowned as she sliced up the ham.

"And you hate camping?" Vinnie asked.

"No, it's not that." She paused a moment thoughtfully. "I just wish he had a dad to do some of these things with, you know, the male-bonding stuff." She shrugged and continued slicing the ham. "But I guess it's important for moms and sons to bond, too."

"What about Charlie? Doesn't he do the male-bonding things with Billy?"

"Sure, but not as often as I'd like. Besides, a grandpa is different from a dad."

"I could do the camping thing with you," Vinnie said. "You know, during the day I can teach Billy the names of plants and how to track animals." He got up and moved to stand just behind her. "I can show him how to make a fire by rubbing two sticks together, make a fishing line with a piece of string and a safety pin." He slid his arms around her, his hands burning imprints into the bare skin of her midriff. "Then at night, while Billy is sleeping, I can sneak into your sleeping bag and make wild, passionate love to you."

"Need I remind you that I only invited you to stay for a sandwich and I have a sharp cutting instrument in my hand?"

He laughed, his breath warm and evocative against her neck. To her relief...and regret, he dropped his hands and moved back to the table.

"Mustard or mayo?" she asked.

Lunch was pleasant. As they ate they spoke of favorite movies and music, discovering common tastes in both. It wasn't until they decided to sit outside and have another glass of iced tea that the talk turned more personal.

"What made you decide that marriage wasn't right for you, Vinnie?" Noreen asked as they sat down in two lawn chairs beneath a shady oak tree.

He was silent for a long moment, his gaze off in the distance. For a brief moment she thought she saw a dark flash of pain flutter in his eyes, but it was gone before she could be certain it had actually been there. Instead his eyes twinkled teasingly. "I just never could see myself tied down to one person for the rest of my life."

Noreen settled back in her chair. "That's where we're different. I grew up seeing my mother and father together, the special relationship they shared, one that deepened with each year. I knew that someday I wanted that for myself."

"You mean that almost psychic connection that lets one person sometimes know what the other is thinking?"

"Exactly," Noreen exclaimed, unaccountably pleased that he knew what she was talking about. "Mom and Dad could say more, express more to each other with a light touch, a soft glance than anyone else I've ever known." She sighed softly. "It was always such a pleasure to be around them."

"And then your mother died and your father is left drifting alone in grief. Doesn't sound like such a terrific thing to me." Vinnie's voice held an edge Noreen had never heard before.

She looked at him in surprise. "It's true. Losing somebody you love hurts, and Dad and I have perhaps wallowed in our hurt for too long. But eventually the hurt fades, and then the heart can be open to trying again. It's human nature to want love."

"Only fools set themselves up for that kind of hurt." His voice was soft, devoid of the teasing tone she'd come to expect from him. He stood up suddenly and gestured toward the tent. "Want me to show you how much fun it is to share a sleeping bag?" he asked.

Noreen gazed at him curiously. "Why do you do that?" she asked.

"Do what?"

"Whenever the conversation gets up-close and personal, you resort to superficial flirting and charming banter."

"That's always been enough to get me what I want."

Noreen studied him a long moment, wondering about the man he kept hidden beneath that charming veneer. "Well, it's not enough this time," she replied softly. "Not nearly enough."

Chapter Eight

Their conversation was interrupted by a voice yelling from the house. "Hey, Mom, where are you?" Billy's voice rang out. Billy exploded out the back door, a smile blossoming across his features as he saw Vinnie. "Hi, Vinnie, did you come to visit me? Are you wearing the medal we won?" Billy pulled his medal from beneath his shirt and displayed it to Vinnie. "I didn't take it off all night."

"Hey, Billy, how ya doing?" Vinnie asked when Billy paused to take a breath.

"Where's Cindy?" Noreen asked.

"She and Jeffrey had to run some errands, then she said she'd be back to drop Jeffrey off," Billy explained. "Jeffrey's spending the night tonight," he said to Vinnie. "Did you see my tent? It's really awesome." He grabbed Vinnie's hand. "Come and let me show you the inside."

"Billy, I don't think Vinnie..." Noreen began.

"It's all right," Vinnie replied. He stood and allowed Billy to pull him toward the canvas structure. Actually, he was glad for the interruption in the conversation with Noreen, a conversation which had suddenly become too personal and uncomfortable.

Billy released Vinnie's hand only long enough to open the flap on the tent, then he once again grasped Vinnie's hand and pulled him inside the stifling little tent.

"Cool, huh?" Billy said as Vinnie sat down on the canvas floor and looked around. "See, there's windows here, and they have screens on them to keep bugs out."

"It's a fine tent, Billy."

The little boy sat cross-legged in front of Vinnie, frowning. "Mom's going to take me camping some time later in the summer. We're going to sleep in here overnight."

"That should be fun," Vinnie said. "Why don't you look happy at the idea?"

Billy looked down, his frown deepening. "When I sleep at night in my room, I have a night-light. Not 'cause I'm scared," he hurriedly added. "I just like the light during the night. But in a tent you can't have a night-light. There's no 'lectricity."

Vinnie smiled. Ah, to be that young again, when a night-light could solve everything, make you feel safe and secure. "I'll tell you a little secret," he said.

"What?" Billy scooted closer to him.

"When I used to go camping, I didn't like the dark, either, so I'd bring a flashlight with me and keep it in my sleeping bag. When I felt like I wanted a little bit of light, I'd just flip on my flashlight.''

Billy smiled at him in relief. ''Yeah, a flashlight, that would be good.'' He threw his arms around Vinnie's neck. For a moment Vinnie held himself stiff, unyielding as he waited for dreadful bittersweet memories to overtake him.

To Vinnie's relief no memories intruded. There was only Billy, who smelled of little-boy sweat and sunshine. He kissed Vinnie's cheek, then released him, his gaze somber.

''If you were my dad, I'd be really, really good,'' Billy said. ''I wouldn't spill my milk at the table, and I'd never talk back.''

The desire, the absolute need in Billy's voice pierced through the armor Vinnie had so carefully erected around his heart. Vinnie's throat thickened with emotion. This kid would be easy to love.

''Come on, let's get out of here before we melt,'' Vinnie said. Together he and Billy crawled out of the tent.

''Want to see my room?'' Billy asked eagerly.

''Another time, sport,'' Vinnie replied. ''I've got to get going.'' He looked at Noreen, who stood from her lawn chair.

''I'll walk you to your car,'' she said, then turned to her son. ''Billy, you'd better get your room picked up before Jeffrey gets here.''

''Bye, Vinnie,'' Billy waved, then disappeared into the house.

''He's a good kid,'' Vinnie said as he and Noreen walked around the house to the front yard.

"Yes, he is," she agreed. "Vinnie...I've decided to have a dinner party. Friday night. Would you come?"

"Why, Noreen, are you asking me out?" he teased.

Her cheeks stained pink. "It's just a dinner party. And before you say yes or no, I'd better warn you, I intend to invite my father and Emily Winston and Cindy and her husband."

He frowned thoughtfully. "What's the occasion?"

She leaned against his car and looked toward Emily's house.

"I've been thinking a lot about what you said yesterday at the picnic, about my father and me hiding out in each other. You were right, and I think it's time I make some changes."

"The chief and Emily Winston...do I smell a matchmaking scheme here?" he asked.

Noreen smiled. "Maybe a little one. Even if they don't actually get together romantically, it would be nice if they could be friends, perhaps companions."

"And you're inviting me because you know no dinner party can truly be successful without my charming presence."

"Not hardly." Her eyes sparkled teasingly. "I need an even number of guests, and until I find Mr. Right you'll have to do."

Vinnie laughed. "Ah, Noreen, nobody will ever accuse you of pumping my ego."

"You seem to pump it fine all by yourself," she observed wryly.

"What time do you want me here Friday?" he asked.

"Seven?"

He nodded and walked around to the driver's side of his car.

"If you're going to do any more painting, don't forget to run a fan."

"Thanks." She backed away from the car, and with a small wave he got in.

As he pulled away from the curb, he watched her in his rearview mirror, wondering what it was about her that so captivated him. Even paint stained, with hair in disarray, she stirred a core of desire inside him.

He loved her humor, that wry, slight sarcasm that perfectly played off his own humor. Bantering with her was nearly as exciting as having sex.

No. He instantly refuted the comparison. He had a feeling making love to Noreen would be earth-shattering...mind numbing.

She would expect and demand complete acquiescence of more than just his body. He had a feeling she would want their spirits to join, their souls to touch.

And Billy. He clenched his hands around the steering wheel as he thought of Billy promising to be a good boy if Vinnie became his father.

Vinnie knew all about growing up hungry for a father. Although his mother had been a loving, wonderful woman, there had been times in his youth when Vinnie had longed for the touch of a big, callused hand, a set of wide shoulders to ride on, a deep male voice whispering a soft good-night. Yes, Vinnie understood Billy's aching need, but it was a need Vinnie couldn't fill.

He wished he could give Noreen and Billy what they wanted, what they deserved, but he couldn't. He'd promised himself a long time ago that he would never again be vulnerable, never again fall in love. And he couldn't allow a freckle-faced kid and a winsome, sexy woman to change his mind.

He parked and walked up the stairs to his second-floor apartment, his thoughts still on Noreen and the conversation Billy had interrupted with his arrival.

He'd known exactly what she'd been talking about when she'd spoken of the special bond, the nonverbal communication that took place between married couples. He'd experienced it firsthand briefly with Valerie. After six years of marriage they'd begun to finish each other's sentences, had often been able to read each other's thoughts.

Oh, their marriage hadn't been perfect. There had been the usual spats that occurred with people living together, loving each other. In fact, that night they'd had a fight, a silly quarrel that had resulted in Vinnie sleeping on the couch…a quarrel that had saved his life while his wife and daughter perished.

He thought of his daughter, Melanie. Sweet Melanie with her bright blue eyes and musical laughter. He sank down on the sofa, allowing his memories of his daughter to wash over him instead of shoving them away as he usually did.

She'd been a bright, loving four-year-old, who loved dancing, a ratty, stuffed rabbit and her daddy. "Daddy's little girl," that's what Valerie had called her from the moment Melanie had been born. She'd come into the world screeching and hollering, quieting only when she'd been placed in Vinnie's arms.

He had a feeling Melanie would have liked Billy. She would have been charmed by his freckles, drawn to his exuberance.

He sighed. There was some comfort in the knowledge Melanie hadn't suffered that night. She'd died in her sleep from smoke inhalation. Although Valerie had been rushed to the hospital, suffering the same, she'd lingered for a day, but had never awakened from a coma.

Vinnie stirred restlessly, his mind suddenly filling with thoughts of his mother, his three sisters. For a long time after the loss of Valerie and Melanie, he shied away from spending time with his family. Seeing his sisters, who'd been best friends with Valerie, brought too much pain. Watching his mother's eyes so filled with grief had simply been too much to bear.

Where bereavement had caused Noreen and her father to cling, grief had made Vinnie distance himself. Now he felt a need to connect.

Before the impulse passed, he picked up his phone and punched in his mother's number. When she answered the phone, a wave of welcomed warmth swept through him and he knew it was the beginning of a healing.

"I don't know why you had to invite him for dinner," Charlie grumbled as he sank down on Noreen's sofa.

"You promised, Dad. You promised you'd be good." Noreen shook a warning finger at him. "If you ruin my dinner party I'll never fix you dinner again.''

Charlie frowned and ran a thumb beneath the collar of his dress shirt. "I'm not going to ruin anything. I just don't understand why you're wasting your time with him.''

"I like him," Noreen answered simply. "He's fun to be around and he makes me laugh.''

"You're dressed awfully pretty for a man who makes you laugh," Charlie commented.

Noreen smiled at the backhanded compliment. "Thanks." She smoothed a hand down the front of the sundress. It had been months since she'd bought anything new to wear and had decided the dinner party was a perfect reason to buy something new. She'd seen the apricot-colored sundress and hadn't been able to resist.

She couldn't remember the last time she'd entertained, and she wanted the evening to be a success. "I need to check on the lasagna," she said, and disappeared into the kitchen.

The air was redolent with the scent of spicy tomato sauce and garlic. After checking the lasagna, she turned down the temperature on the oven then inspected the table to make sure it was set with everything necessary.

She'd gone all out, unpacking her mother's china and using it for the first time in years. Bright red cloth napkins added festive color to the white dinnerware, and candles in the center of the table awaited a touch of a match.

"Everything looks real nice," Charlie said from

the doorway. "But I thought you said there were going to be six of us." He looked at the table set for four.

"Cindy and her husband couldn't make it, so it will just be the four of us."

"It sure smells good." He shifted from foot to foot and once again ran a finger beneath his collar.

Noreen smiled at him. She realized the big man who'd faced deadly situations and braved fires for a living was nervous. She reached up and touched his cheek lightly. "I have it on good authority that Emily Winston won't bite," she said.

"I know that. Emily and I went to high school together."

The conversation was interrupted by the ringing of the doorbell. Noreen hurried to answer it, finding Vinnie on her front porch. Clad in a pair of black dress slacks and a gray shirt, he looked more handsome than Noreen could ever remember.

"Wow. You look terrific," he said as he stepped inside, his gaze warm as it slid down the length of her.

"You clean up pretty nice yourself," she returned lightly.

"These are for you." He held out a bouquet of flowers, their sweet perfume filling the air between them.

"Thank you." She took the bouquet, touched by his gesture.

"Is Billy here?"

"No, he's spending the night with a friend."

"I've got something for him, too." He held out a

flashlight with an action figure handle. She looked at him curiously. He smiled. "He'll know what it's for. Hi, Chief." Vinnie greeted Charlie, who stepped into the living room from the kitchen.

"Pastorelli." Charlie nodded and sank down on the sofa.

"Please, make yourself at home while I go put these in some water." As Noreen passed her father, she shot him a warning glare.

As she placed the flowers in a vase of water, she heard no conversation coming from the living room. This was probably a mistake, she thought. Inviting Vinnie and her father over on the same night. She understood her father's worry about her relationship with Vinnie. He'd been at her side, seen her destruction when Jesse had left her.

But he had to understand that she was an adult and would make her own choices where companions were concerned. She had to make her own mistakes…not that she intended to make a mistake with Vinnie.

She carried the flowers back out to the living room, where the two men sat at opposite sides of the room staring off into space. "Here we are," she said as she set the vase in the center of the coffee table. "They're beautiful, aren't they?"

Charlie grunted and Vinnie merely smiled. Noreen wanted to box both their ears. "Would either of you like a glass of wine?"

"Sure," Charlie replied.

"Sounds great," Vinnie agreed.

Noreen returned to the kitchen and grabbed a bottle of red wine. Again silence reigned in the living room.

Drat the two of them. They worked together nearly every day. Surely they could figure out some safe topic of conversation.

She'd just served them the wine when the doorbell rang again, announcing Emily's arrival. Noreen breathed a sigh of relief, hoping the older woman's presence would loosen up the two men.

Emily had obviously dressed with special care. Her dress was a powder blue that emphasized the blue of her eyes and a touch of blush colored her cheeks, matching the shade of her lipstick.

Both Vinnie and Charlie stood as she entered. As usual, she carried a pie. "Lemon meringue," she said as she handed it to Noreen.

"Mrs. Winston, can I get you a glass of wine?" Vinnie asked.

"Oh, that sounds nice. But, please, call me Emily, dear."

Vinnie followed Noreen into the kitchen, leaving Charlie and Emily alone in the living room. As Noreen placed the pie in the refrigerator, Vinnie grabbed the bottle of wine.

She closed the refrigerator and turned around, a gasp escaping her as Vinnie stepped up to within inches of where she stood. He reached up a finger and lightly traced the line of her jaw. "You look absolutely ravishing in that dress," he said softly.

"I'm glad you like it," she replied, fighting the urge to turn her face into his caress.

"You know what I've been thinking about ever since the picnic?" he asked.

"What?" The single word escaped from her on a whisper of anticipation.

"This." He lowered his head and lightly brushed his lips against hers.

Noreen's response was instantaneous. Her breath quickened and her pulse raced. As Vinnie's mouth left hers and trailed hot kisses down her neck, she took a step away from him. "Vinnie, my dad is in the next room."

"I know, but I'm not interested in kissing him," he murmured against her throat.

She giggled and gave him a light push. "Be nice," she chided. "Take Emily her glass of wine while I broil the garlic toast."

"Okay, but later, when the old folks go home, I intend to be really nice to you." He winked teasingly and she laughed again.

"Go on, get out of here."

She was still smiling as she prepared the garlic toast and popped it into the oven. She'd forgotten how much fun the chase could be, and she was enjoying it as much as Vinnie was.

As she waited for the bread to brown, she relaxed as she heard the muted sound of conversation going on in the living room. As she heard her dad's burst of laughter, she was certain this little gathering had been a good idea.

Minutes later they all gathered around the table for the dinner Noreen had prepared. "Everything looks wonderful," Emily said as she unfolded her napkin and placed it in her lap.

"Noreen's a great cook. She learned from her

mother." Charlie fumbled with his napkin, his eyes downcast.

"Did Noreen also inherit her mother's fondness for dancing?" Emily asked.

Charlie looked up at Emily in surprise. "You remember how much Carolyn loved to dance?"

"Oh, my, yes. I remember at the school dances you and Carolyn could really cut a rug." Emily smiled at Noreen. "I'll bet you didn't know your father was voted most likely to be a movie star."

Charlie laughed, a deep blush sweeping over his face and reddening the tips of his ears. "That was a long time ago."

"Yes, it was. But there's been a lot of good times in between," Emily replied.

"Yeah, there has," Charlie agreed, his eyes losing some of the darkness they'd held for the last four years. He looked at Noreen and Vinnie. "Well, what are we waiting for. Let's eat."

They ate and talked and laughed. Emily and Charlie entertained Noreen and Vinnie with old stories about themselves and other people they'd gone to school with.

Any tension that had initially swelled between Charlie and Vinnie dissipated at the table amid the shared laughter. Although Noreen wasn't fool enough to expect this dinner to change the way Charlie felt about Vinnie, she was grateful for the momentary truce that existed.

It was difficult to concentrate on the conversation going on when Vinnie sat next to her, his thigh touching hers, occasionally pressing against hers, unmistakably not by accident.

The candlelight did wonderful things to his features, emphasizing the darkness of his hair and eyes, playing on the angles and planes of his handsome face. He smiled at her, his smile so warm, so tender it nearly stole her breath away.

She looked away, suddenly afraid of the feelings he evoked in her. It was supposed to be a game…he was supposed to be a game, just fun until she found a man who wanted commitment, wanted the kind of life she did. But it no longer felt like a game. It felt more than a little bit frightening.

"Who's ready for dessert and coffee?" She stood up, needing some activity, something physical to take her mind off the emotions that seemed too confusing at the moment.

"I am," Charlie answered, and looked at Emily with something approaching fondness. "What about you, Emily?"

She shook her head. "I'll pass on the dessert, but coffee sounds good."

"Just coffee for me, too." Vinnie's eyes shone wickedly. "Maybe I'll have a little dessert later."

Dessert was just as pleasant as the meal had been. Vinnie told several tales about his lawyering days, amusing anecdotes that had them all reeling with laughter.

"What made you decide to stop being a lawyer and become a fireman?" Emily asked the question that had been on the tip of Noreen's tongue.

Vinnie shrugged and stared down into his coffee

for a long moment. "I needed a change of pace. You might say I was burned out." They all groaned at his pun and he grinned. "Although I must confess there are days—" he shot a sly glance at Charlie "—especially lately when I've been spending a lot of time waxing and polishing Big Red, that I think fondly of those days of desk sitting and paperwork."

Charlie cleared his throat. "Nothing wrong with polishing the rig," he exclaimed.

"I have a feeling I'll be doing it a lot in the future, as well," Vinnie replied, his eyes not wavering from Charlie.

Charlie laughed, a touch of admiration in his eyes. "You're a stubborn cuss, Pastorelli."

"I think there's probably more than one of those in this room," Emily said sweetly, causing both men to roar with laughter.

"Why don't you three take your coffee into the living room and I'll join you in just a moment," Noreen suggested as she started to clear the dirty dishes from the table.

"Here, I'll help you with those," Emily said. "Go, you men go on in the living room." She shooed them out of the kitchen. "This has been such a lovely evening," she said to Noreen as she gathered several plates and carried them to the sink.

"It has been nice, hasn't it?" Noreen smiled. "I can't remember the last time Dad laughed so much."

"He's a good man," Emily said, her cheeks a little more pink than usual.

"You like him, don't you?" Noreen knew the answer by the deepening blush on Emily's face.

"I've always admired your father." She laughed and raised her hands to her cheeks. "Look at me, you have me blushing like a schoolgirl."

Noreen laughed and gave her a quick hug. "I think he likes you, too."

For a few minutes the two women worked in companionable silence, putting the dishes in the dishwasher and tidying up the rest of the kitchen.

A sense of contentment filled Noreen as she worked. Even if nothing romantic transpired between Charlie and Emily, she knew this night was a big step for her father, and that he and Emily would at least become friends. It was enough for now.

Noreen placed the last plate in the dishwasher. "Thanks for the help, Emily." She turned to see the older woman clutching the edge of the table with one hand, her chest with the other. Her face was whitened and twisted in pain. "Emily!"

"I...I..." Emily's breaths came fast, as if she couldn't draw enough air.

"Here...sit down." Noreen pulled out a chair. "Dad! Vinnie!" she yelled.

Emily slumped to the floor as the two men raced into the room.

Chapter Nine

"Call 911," Vinnie said to Charlie.

As Charlie ran to the phone, Vinnie sank down on the floor next to Emily. Her eyes blinked rapidly, and her hands still clutched her chest.

Vinnie took one of her hands in his. "You're okay, Emily. You're going to be just fine. Hold my hand...that's right. You keep squeezing my hand." His voice was soft, soothing.

Noreen hovered nearby, realizing there was nothing she could do to help. "An ambulance is on its way," Charlie said as he hung up the phone.

"Hear that, sweetheart? You hang on and help will be here in just a minute." Vinnie smiled at Emily. "This is all my fault. I was probably just too darn charming for your ticker, right?"

A faint smile fluttered at the corner of Emily's lips despite the tears that oozed slowly down her cheeks.

It was at that moment Noreen realized she loved

Vinnie. As she listened to him sweet-talking Emily, yet saw the deep concern and caring that radiated from his eyes, she knew this man had somehow managed to crawl beneath her defenses, despite her resolve to the contrary.

There was no time to contemplate the discovery of this new emotion. Within minutes the ambulance had arrived and paramedics filled the kitchen. Emily was whisked to the waiting vehicle on a stretcher.

Vinnie remained at her side, crawling into the back of the ambulance to ride to the hospital with her. Charlie and Noreen followed in Charlie's car.

It took them only a few minutes to reach the hospital and park the car. When they reached the Emergency waiting room, Vinnie was already there.

"How's she doing?" Noreen asked, Charlie at her side.

"Doctors are with her now. Somebody will come out and tell us as soon as they know something." He took Noreen's hand, his gaze warm yet concerned. "She remained conscious, that's a good sign."

Charlie motioned to the plastic chairs against one wall. "We might as well get comfortable. It will probably be a while before we know anything."

Together the three of them sank down in the chairs, Noreen between the two worried men. "There was no warning," Noreen said softly. "One minute she was just fine and the next she was clutching her chest." She grimaced and laced and unlaced her fingers in her lap. "I should have insisted she not help with the dishes. I should have made her sit at the table until I was finished. I know she has a heart condition."

"Emily would never forgive you if you treated her like an invalid," Charlie replied.

"He's right," Vinnie agreed as his hand reached over to grasp hers.

She clung to his hand tightly, grateful to have something to hang on to. Emily's collapse had frightened her, and until that moment she hadn't realized just how much she'd come to care for the older woman.

For the last four years, since her mother's death, the dignified, quietly supportive neighbor had helped fill a void in Noreen's life. She squeezed Vinnie's hand, closed her eyes and sent a prayer upward.

They sat silent for nearly half an hour before a doctor came out to inform them Emily was being taken directly into surgery for a heart bypass operation. He encouraged them to go home, that the operation would take several hours and there was nothing they could do sitting in the waiting room.

"You two go on home and get some rest," Noreen said when the doctor had disappeared. "There's no point in all of us staying here. Billy is gone for the night, so I'll stay and let you both know when she's out of surgery."

"I don't mind staying. I don't have to work tomorrow," Vinnie said.

"But, Dad, you do have to work in the morning." Noreen looked at her father, saw the lines of strain that creased his face. She suddenly realized this was probably the first time Charlie had been in a hospital since her mother's death.

"I should stay at least until she gets out of the

operating room and we know she's all right," Charlie replied.

"You heard the doctor…that could be hours. I can call you the minute we know something." Noreen placed a hand on her dad's arm. "Go home, Dad. I'll let you know what happens."

Charlie hesitated. "You promise you'll call?"

"I promise," Noreen agreed.

"Okay." He raked a hand through his hair, then leaned down and kissed Noreen on the cheek. "If you get a chance to see her before I do…tell her I had a good time tonight." He gave Noreen a quick hug, then turned and left.

"Why don't we go downstairs to the cafeteria and get a cup of coffee?" Vinnie suggested when Charlie had gone.

"You don't have to stay, Vinnie."

"You're right, I don't have to, but I want to." He took her by the arm. "Come on, I hear the coffee here is absolutely horrendous. Tourists come from miles around just to taste how bad it is."

Noreen smiled. "How can I refuse an offer like that?"

The hospital cafeteria was nearly empty. A nurse sat alone reading a newspaper at one table, and an older couple held hands across another table, obviously supporting one another through one of life's dramas.

Vinnie and Noreen got their drinks, then sat down at a table in the corner.

"I hate hospitals," Vinnie said.

"I don't know too many people who like them," Noreen replied.

"To me they always smell like pain and loss."

Noreen looked at him in surprise. He stared down into his coffee cup, a knot of muscle in his jaw pulsing with tension. He gazed up at her, for a brief moment his eyes radiating a dark inner pain.

He blinked, instantly dispelling the emotion and replacing it with an easy grin. "Guess the smell of antiseptic will never be an aphrodisiac for me."

Noreen wanted to explore the reason for that brief darkness in his eyes, one of the few genuine emotions she'd ever seen from him. But she knew now was not the time nor the place. "Good things happen in hospitals, too. People are healed and babies are born."

"Don't tell Billy about the babies. He'll be down here instantly to try to get one."

Noreen laughed, knowing it was true. She sipped her coffee and gazed over at the older couple, hands still clasped across the table. She looked back at Vinnie. "I'm glad you stayed with me. The waiting is always easier if it's shared."

Warmth flooded through her as he reached across the table and covered her hand with his. "I wouldn't have it any other way," he said softly.

With the comfort of his hand on hers, Noreen realized again that somehow this man had managed to get to her. Despite her determination to the contrary, he'd pierced through the layers of protection to lay claim to her heart.

She didn't want it, knew she couldn't rely on it. He'd made it clear from the very beginning he was a confirmed bachelor, not material for marriage and fatherhood.

She pulled her hand from beneath his and wrapped it around her mug. She didn't want to think about her feelings for him right now. She'd sort them out later, come to her senses after she was assured of Emily's condition.

"You were right about the coffee. It is horrendous," she said, breaking the silence that had grown between them.

He grinned. "It's one of the few things in life you can count on...that the coffee in a hospital will be awful."

She tried to return his grin, but to her horror tears blurred her vision and a sob choked her throat. The trauma of the last hour caught up to her, and she felt her control slipping away.

"Hey." Vinnie moved from his chair across from her and into the one right next to her. Without hesitation he opened his arms and pulled her into an embrace. "She's going to be all right," he said softly as his hand stroked the length of Noreen's hair.

"She's just so good...so nice. It isn't fair," Noreen gasped out.

"I know, I know. But sometimes bad things happen to good people and it's nobody's fault. They just happen."

The warmth of his comfort, the tenderness in his touch only served to make Noreen's tears fall faster. The shock of Emily's attack, combined with the frantic fear as they'd waited for help, now sought the cathartic release through tears.

Vinnie seemed to sense her need for this release. He patted her back and held her close against his chest. "It's all right," he said softly. "That's it, let it out. Let it all out."

And she did. She cried tears of fear for Emily. She released emotion that had been bottled up for too long. Finally she cried for herself, for being stupid enough to fall in love with a man whose arms surrounded her with comfort.

The front of his shirt smelled clean and fresh, and his arms offered a sweet warmth she wanted to remain in forever. She finally pulled herself away from him, embarrassed by her tears and needing to distance herself from the pleasure of his embrace.

"Sorry," she said as she wrapped her hands around her coffee mug.

"Don't be. Without tears the soul wouldn't have rainbows."

"Did you just make that up?"

He grinned, the charming smile she loved and wished she could somehow get beneath. "Nah, it was something Emily said to me."

"She's such a wonderful woman." Noreen frowned worriedly. "I wonder what's going on? Maybe we should go back upstairs to the waiting room and see if there's any other news."

"Okay," he agreed.

As they went back to the waiting room, Vinnie placed an arm around her shoulders. Although she knew he was the wrong man for her, she was grateful for his comfort, his strength and support at the moment.

There was no news. The nurse behind the desk informed them that Emily was still in surgery but that's all the information she had.

Noreen and Vinnie returned to the chairs they'd been sitting in before, only this time Vinnie kept his arm around Noreen and she rested her head on his shoulder.

A large-faced clock hung opposite them on the wall. Noreen watched the second hand ticking off minutes. "It's going to be a long night, isn't it?" she said softly.

Vinnie squeezed her shoulder in comfort. "Yeah, I'm afraid it is."

In the next several hours the silence of the Emergency Room was broken only occasionally. Young parents with a sick child, a man who'd cut himself while opening a can...it seemed to be an unusually quiet night for emergencies in Ridgeview.

Vinnie was grateful. By midnight Noreen slept against his shoulder, her warm, even breath lightly fanning his neck. His arm behind her had gone to sleep an hour before, but he didn't mind the discomfort. He knew the easiest way for her to pass an anxious wait was in sleep.

He wished he could sleep, but he was afraid the all-too-familiar smell of the hospital, the memory of those hours of sitting up with Valerie, would evoke unwanted nightmares.

Instead he focused on the simple pleasure of holding Noreen. Her hair smelled fresh, and it lay against his arm like a soft sheet of silk. Her hands rested in her lap, dainty, with fingers slightly curled, oddly vulnerable looking.

Although she'd clung to him as she'd cried, all soft need, he knew she was a strong woman. For the past four years she'd raised her son alone, and Vinnie knew what kind of strength that took, knew by his own fatherless childhood.

He smiled, remembering the phone conversation he'd shared with his mother. He was glad he'd called. He'd allowed his grief to close him off from all he cared about. He'd ended the conversation promising not only to stay in touch with her, but to call his sisters, as well.

Family. That's what Billy wanted with his desire for a baby. The feeling of family, of being connected to something bigger than yourself. Vinnie'd had that once, and while he'd bridged the gap with his extended family, he never wanted to be vulnerable again with a nuclear family of his own.

Noreen deserved a whole man, somebody who could give her and Billy all his heart, all his soul. Not a man like himself, whose heart was covered in the ashes of his wife and child's death.

It was nearing two o'clock when the doctor finally appeared in the waiting room, his face creased with deep lines of weariness. Vinnie nudged Noreen awake, and together they rose to greet the doctor.

"She came through fine," he said without preamble.

Noreen sagged in relief against Vinnie's side. "Can we see her?" she asked.

"She'll be in recovery for quite some time," the

doctor explained. "I suggest you both go home and visit her later when she's moved to a room of her own."

"Thank you. Thank you for taking such good care of her," Noreen said, and Vinnie nodded his agreement.

It wasn't until they walked out of the hospital and into the warm, still, night air that they realized they didn't have a way to get home.

"We could always hijack an ambulance and drive ourselves home," Noreen joked.

"I could go back inside and call us a cab," Vinnie offered.

Noreen looked down the tree-lined sidewalk where they stood. "We're only twelve or fifteen blocks from my house. It's a beautiful night, and I'm so wound up. Let's walk it."

"Sounds good," Vinnie agreed easily.

As they started down the sidewalk, he captured her hand in his. The half-moon slice overhead radiated just enough illumination for her features to be visible. He was grateful to see the tension that had tugged at her features earlier was gone, replaced by the knowledge that Emily would be all right.

"I'll say one thing for you, Noreen. You sure know how to give an exciting dinner party."

She laughed, the melodic sound filling the quiet night air and bringing a responsive smile to his lips. "I hope I never give one that turns out with this much excitement again." She looked at him, her eyes glowing almost silver in the moonlight. "Vinnie, thanks again for tonight. I'm glad you were there for me."

"That's what friends are for," he returned. She squeezed his hand.

They fell into a pleasant silence and continued walking. Around them it seemed the entire world was asleep. No dogs barked, no cars passed to break the aura of peaceful quiet.

"Just think," he said. "In some of these houses, in the darkness of night, new lovers are discovering the joys of each other at this very moment."

She shot him a wry smile. "Of course you would think of lovers and not husbands and wives."

He grinned. "Husbands and wives aren't making love. They're fighting over the blankets or snoring in exhaustion, and maybe wishing they could once again find the passion, the fire that had once brought them together."

She elbowed him in the ribs. "You're a terrible cynic," she exclaimed as he grabbed his ribs in mock injury. She stopped walking and eyed him intently. "Sometimes I think you're just trying to fool everyone into thinking you're so cynical, and the person you're most wanting to convince is yourself."

He laughed, strangely discomfited by her words. "I think it's far too early in the morning for you to be psychoanalyzing me."

"You're absolutely right." She grabbed his arm, and they continued on.

Something had changed between them. Vinnie wasn't sure how or why, but her guard seemed to be down. She seemed more open to him, and it both aroused him and confused him.

Surely it was just a combination of the drama the

night had brought, the worry they'd shared and the comfort they'd sought in each other. It couldn't be that she was getting in too deep with him, that she was forgetting his rules, forgetting how wrong he was for her.

He rubbed a hand down his face, deciding he was overthinking. It had been a long night, and he was getting punchy, imagining things.

Lights spilled from Noreen's windows as they approached the house. Vinnie felt an odd sense of homecoming at the sight of the well-lit home amid the darkness of the night. His car was parked in the driveway…looking like it belonged there.

Pressure filled his chest and he swallowed hard against it. "So, you going to invite me in to see your etchings?" he asked, striving for the light flirting where he'd always found comfort.

She withdrew her keys from her purse, unlocked her front door then turned and gazed at him, her eyes the warm blue of a summer sky. "It's late, Vinnie, and I'm exhausted." She smiled and to his surprise reached up and kissed him on the cheek. She tilted her head to one side, as if making up her mind about something. "If you were to ask me out on a date again, maybe this time I'd say yes."

Surprise winged through him, along with a flurry of anticipation. He smoothed a strand of hair from her face, noting the endearing sprinkle of freckles across her nose. "How about next Saturday night…dinner and dancing and maybe a peek at your etchings?"

Her lips curved up in a smile of utter invitation.

"What time?" The question whispered out of her with breathless expectation.

He accepted the invitation on her lips, covering them with his own. She returned his kiss sweetly, openly, and Vinnie felt her heart beating against his own. It was the rhythm of something more than desire. It beat a steady pulse of tenderness and caring.

He broke the kiss. "Seven o'clock next Saturday," he said. He touched her cheek one last time, then turned and headed for his car.

It wasn't until he pulled into his own drive that he realized—in agreeing to go out with him, Noreen had given him far more than just a yes to a simple date.

He realized she'd given him her heart.

Now all he had to do was figure out what he intended to do with it.

Chapter Ten

"**Y**ou look wonderful," Noreen said to Emily the following afternoon. The older woman looked tiny in the hospital bed, but her hair was neatly combed and a pale pink lipstick covered her mouth. It would be easy to forget what she'd just been through if not for the intravenous tubes that were connected to her.

Although Emily's face was still pale, her eyes danced with life as Noreen pulled a chair up next to the bed. "How are you feeling?"

"Surprisingly well." Emily shook her head, a touch of wonder on her features. "It's amazing, isn't it? What can be done medically now. Last night I thought for sure the pearly gates were opening wide just for me, and this morning the doctor said I'll probably be home in a week."

"That's great news," Noreen replied.

Emily reached out one hand and grabbed one of

Noreen's. "I'm sorry I gave you such a scare last night."

Noreen laughed and squeezed her hand affectionately. "Let's just say you know how to make a dramatic exit. Can I bring you anything? Things from home?"

"No, dear, I'm fine. The staff here is absolutely wonderful."

Noreen looked around the room, spying a splendid bouquet of flowers on a desk in the corner. "Looks like somebody has already sent you flowers."

Emily nodded, faint pink color stealing into her cheeks. "Your father had those delivered first thing this morning." Noreen looked at her in surprise.

"He also sent a little note telling me that when I'm up to it he'll take me dancing." The color in Emily's cheeks deepened. "He said he remembered I was a fine dancer at one time, and he wants to see if there's still some rhythm left in me." Emily frowned suddenly. "You don't mind, do you? I mean, I would never attempt to take your mother's place with Charlie or with you."

"Mind? Oh, Emily, I can't think of anything nicer than the two people I care most about caring for each other."

Emily shifted positions, wincing slightly, then smiled at Noreen. "Your mother would have been so proud of you, Noreen. She was a woman with a heart as big as the mountains, and you're so much like her."

A bittersweet pain swelled up inside her at Emily's words. "A day doesn't go by that I don't miss her."

Emily nodded. "I feel that way about my husband. But the living must go on living, and I'm pleased to see that you've rediscovered your laughter, seemed to have renewed your hope. It's that young man of yours, Vinnie. He's good for you."

It was Noreen's turn to blush. Her cheeks warmed at thoughts of Vinnie, the comfort they had shared, the kiss that had stolen her breath. "Yes, Vinnie makes me laugh," she answered. And he makes me want him. He makes me wish for things I shouldn't. Her cheeks flamed hotter with her inner thoughts.

Once again Emily reached for her hand. "And I think you're good for him, too." Her eyes fluttered tiredly. "Somewhere beneath that charming patter of his is a heart that's been sorely wounded." She closed her eyes. "I don't know what caused his pain, but I'm old enough to recognize it when I see it."

Noreen waited a moment for Emily to continue, then realized she'd fallen asleep. Gently Noreen removed her hand from the older woman's, then stood and quietly left the room.

As she drove home from the hospital, she thought of Emily's words. Certainly Emily's perception that Vinnie was hiding some sort of inner pain corresponded with the same feelings Noreen had gotten at odd moments with the handsome man.

That moment when he'd touched the side of his car and his eyes had darkened in pain…then last night with his talk of hospitals and death. Was it possible that whatever might have happened in his past was what made him so cynical, so afraid of love now?

She scoffed at these thoughts, unable to imagine Vinnie afraid of anything.

Saturday night. A date with Vinnie. She shivered at the thought, knowing that for her the night would be far more than a date. She'd effectively agreed to make love to him, to allow herself to be utterly vulnerable once again. The thought both terrified her and thrilled her.

Although Vinnie had made it clear with words that he wanted no commitment, his actions had been more ambivalent. There was genuine caring in his touch, tenderness in his eyes. Surely he couldn't manufacture those emotions merely for the pleasure of seducing her into his bed.

She loved him, and there was no going back from that. She loved him, and she was leaving her heart open to fate's whims as to whether she would finally find happiness or if she would only be hurt once again.

"Mom!" Billy greeted her as she parked in the driveway. He and Jeffrey were playing in the flower bed with their miniature trucks and cars. "How's Mrs. Winston?" he asked.

"She's doing terrific. Where's Cindy?"

The boys pointed inside and resumed their play.

Noreen found Cindy at the kitchen table thumbing through a magazine. She looked up as Noreen walked in. "Hey, how's Emily?"

"Fine." Noreen went to the refrigerator and grabbed a can of soda. "She says she should be home in a week."

Cindy closed her magazine and shoved it aside.

"I'm sorry Adam and I weren't here last night to help out. We had a boring, stiff, business dinner to attend."

"It's just as well you weren't here," Noreen said truthfully. "More people would have only added to the chaos."

"So, how did it go before Emily got ill?"

Noreen smiled and sank down at the table. "A little stiff at first. Dad and Vinnie seemed to be playing a game where the loser was the first one to say something nice to each other. They both loosened up once Emily arrived."

"That's nice, but I really don't care about how Vinnie and your father got along. I want to know about you and Vinnie."

Noreen smiled at her best friend. "I have a date with him for next Saturday night."

Cindy nodded, her eyes lighting with excitement. "A date. As in a real date?"

Noreen laughed. "Yes, a real date."

"I knew there was something special between the two of you. I knew it the first time I saw you together. I told you before...sparks flew."

Noreen shrugged, feigning a nonchalance she didn't feel. "It's just a date."

"We've been friends too long, Noreen, for me to believe it's 'just' a date."

Any pretense of nonchalance fell away. "I'm in love with him," Noreen whispered, as if to say the words any louder frightened her. She took a drink of her soda, then continued. "Heaven knows I didn't want to love him. I fought against it every step of the way.''

"But the heart rarely listens to the head,'' Cindy replied.

Noreen wrapped her hands around the coolness of the soda can and frowned. ''I let my heart guide me once before, and it was the biggest mistake of my life.''

"But Vinnie and Jesse are not the same men.''

Noreen nodded. ''I know that, but Vinnie has never led me to believe that he wants to be anything but a bachelor.''

Cindy snorted. ''Every single man in the world professes the same thing until some woman changes their mind. You just have to be sure you're the woman who changes Vinnie's mind.''

As Saturday night approached, Noreen played and replayed Cindy's words in her mind. She didn't want to change Vinnie's mind. She simply wanted him to want her as she wanted him...forever. And she thought...she believed there was a possibility of that.

He called her on Thursday, confirming their date, but he called from the station and so had no time to talk. Still, the sound of his voice filled her with warmth, with a wild anticipation for their approaching date.

Saturday Noreen was too nervous to sit around the house and wait for seven o'clock to arrive. With Billy at Cindy's for the night and far too many hours until Vinnie was due to arrive, she decided to shop for a special dress to wear that evening.

She began at noon and didn't get back home until

almost five, new dress, shoes and underclothes in bags. Her hands shook as she started her bath water and added a liberal dose of fragrant bath crystals.

It was ridiculous to be so nervous, silly to feel like a teenage girl anticipating her very first date. But she couldn't quell the nerves that jumped and danced in her tummy.

She'd bought sinfully sexy underclothes, unlike any she'd ever purchased before. She could easily imagine the desire in Vinnie's eyes as he saw the pale blue silk chemise and tiny matching panties. A delicious shiver worked up her spine despite the warmth of the surrounding water.

Sinking deeper into the tub, she contemplated the evening to come. Vinnie. She closed her eyes and allowed his features to dance across her mind. His laughter warmed her. His wit tickled her. As she'd watched him running the race with Billy at the firemen's picnic, her heart had expanded with emotion. When he'd kissed her that first time, she'd known a passion she'd never felt before.

And as he'd held her in the hospital as they'd waited for news about Emily, she'd known a pureness of love, a sense of belonging.

She loved him. With every fiber of her being, with every beat of her heart. She loved him. And she was helpless against it, defenseless with him.

What had begun as fun, as a game of harmless flirting and teasing had, for her, transformed into something so deep, so profoundly important. Surely he'd come to know her well enough to realize this fact.

She only hoped and prayed it wasn't still just a game for Vinnie.

Vinnie knew the moment he awakened on Saturday morning that he would not, could not keep his date that evening with Noreen.

He slept late, having suffered nightmares all night long and finally falling into a merciful, dreamless sleep of exhaustion near dawn.

The moment he opened his eyes, he knew what day it was...not Saturday, not a glorious day in late June, but rather the anniversary of the day his life fell apart.

Exactly two years ago he'd lost his wife and his child. His chest tightened as he waited for the knots of grief to rip him apart. Vaguely he was surprised when the intensity of the grief was less than he'd expected.

Maybe time was finally healing the hurt. When it had happened, everyone had told him time would take care of the pain, but he hadn't believed them. And now the pain was finally becoming manageable.

He'd been stupid to make the date for today, stupid to make the date at all.

He cared about Noreen. If he allowed it, he knew he'd find love for her in his heart. But, he didn't want to find it. He never wanted to hurt again like he'd hurt when he'd lost Valerie and Melanie.

It was far easier to keep things on the surface, to not allow emotions to get too deep, go too far. That's what he'd been doing for the last two years, keeping things on the surface, but now Noreen threatened to change all that. And he couldn't let it happen.

As soon as he was up and showered, he called a travel agent and arranged for a flight to Chicago. He'd leave this afternoon and return tomorrow afternoon. He needed to be there, at the cemetery, place flowers on their graves and remember the love they'd once all shared.

Once the travel arrangements were made, he tried to call Noreen. No answer, and she was one of the few women left in the world who didn't own an answering machine.

He tried to call several more times without getting her before his three-o'clock flight. Finally he couldn't put it off any longer. If he was going to make his plane, he had to leave.

It wasn't until he was on the plane, soaring away from Ridgeview and back to his past, that he wondered if perhaps subconsciously he hadn't sabotaged his growing feelings for Noreen by making a date he couldn't keep.

This anniversary date hadn't exactly sneaked up on him. He'd known it was coming…dreaded it for days.

But going out with Noreen would be like turning his back on his past, forgetting about the wife and daughter he'd loved…and lost.

He stared unseeing out the window, where fluffy white clouds obscured the earth below. And in those clouds he saw Noreen's face, so open, so giving as she'd agreed to the date with him. Her smile, so genuine and warm, those eyes that bewitched and bedeviled him, each and every feature was etched in his mind.

She'd never forgive him for this. Vinnie had no

illusions about that. Noreen had offered him her heart, her trust by agreeing to the date. He was breaking her trust by standing her up.

Maybe it's best this way, he thought, tearing his gaze from the window and to the in-flight magazine in his lap. Maybe it was best that she hate him, that she never again be tempted to talk to him, flirt with him.

He'd find another woman to spend time with, one who didn't touch his heart so profoundly, one who wasn't a threat.

Yes, it was best that she move on and he do the same. No sense in continuing to see each other, when the end result would only be her being hurt more deeply than she already was.

He wasn't the man for her, and in standing her up, in abusing the trust she'd handed him, he was only proving what she'd already known, that he was a flirting fool, but not a good bet for forever.

Noreen didn't start feeling sick to her stomach until seven-thirty. He's just a half hour late, she thought as she stood at the window watching for his car.

Okay, so maybe punctuality wasn't a strong suit of his.

She'd been known to be tardy for appointments before. She could forgive his lateness.

She left the front window and walked to her bedroom. Standing in the doorway, she stared at the room that had been transformed over the past week.

The room still held a faint scent of new paint, a smell that now mingled with the scent of the perfume she'd used earlier and the fragrance of the flower bouquet next to the bed.

She'd bought the flowers that day, their joyous colors reflecting the joy in her heart as she anticipated the night with Vinnie. She closed her eyes, able to imagine herself and Vinnie tangled in the sheets of the bed, the sweet floral fragrance surrounding them as they made slow, delicious love.

Frowning, she looked at her watch. Seven forty-five. "Where are you, Vinnie?" she mumbled as she walked back into the living room and over to the window once again, expecting to see the lights of his car at any moment.

Vinnie. She smiled as she thought of him. Vinnie with his devastating smile and those dark eyes that smoldered desire.

Visions of the future filled her head. A future of love, of happiness, visions of a real family. Like the flowers in the bedroom, Noreen had bloomed with hope, blossomed with the promise of the future. All she needed was Vinnie to arrive, for her future to be at hand.

By eight-fifteen the sickness in her stomach intensified, and for the first time she wondered if he was going to show up at all. What would cause him not to show?

A blonde?

A redhead?

She shoved those thoughts aside, aware that they were residual baggage left over from Jesse. Maybe a fire had broken out...an enormous fire that had prompted the dispatcher to call in all the men. It had happened before, two years ago when a warehouse on the south side of town had gone up in blazes. Not only had every man in the department worked to stanch the flames, but dozens of townspeople pitched in, as well.

Stepping out on the front porch, she looked first one way, then the other, seeking a glow that would signify such a fire. Nothing but stars overhead and no other illumination that would point to a huge fire. Despite the warmth of the night breeze, a cold chill swept through her heart.

He wasn't coming.

She wrapped her arms around her shoulders, the chill intensifying with each breath she took, every moment that passed. An hour and a half late. No, not late. He wasn't going to show up.

Tilting her head back, she stared at the moon overhead, unsurprised when it blurred and swam as tears filled her eyes. She swiped at her eyes, amazed that her tears could be so hot when she was so cold within.

It had all been a game to him. Nothing more. And what a challenge she'd presented, refusing to go out with him. A challenge a player would find most desirable.

She turned and went back into the house, tearing off the new dress as she stumbled toward her bedroom. She'd been a fool. Such an enormous fool.

The taste of bitterness filled her mouth, along with the acrid flavor of unshed tears. She dropped the dress on the bedroom floor and yanked off the sexy, silky underclothes.

She pulled on a pair of sturdy white cotton underpants, then got into the oversize T-shirt she wore to bed. How could she have been such a fool? Her father had tried to warn her about Vinnie. Why hadn't she listened?

Before crawling into bed she took the flowers she'd bought earlier in the day and dumped them in the trash. That's what Vinnie had done to her heart. He'd courted it, won it, then tossed it away like garbage.

He was the ultimate game player and he'd won. His prize...her broken heart.

Chapter Eleven

By the time Vinnie returned from Chicago late on Sunday afternoon, he decided Noreen deserved some sort of explanation for being stood up the night before.

The evening before he'd stood at the cemetery in front of where his daughter and wife rested, and he'd thought about the two of them...and Noreen and Billy. He'd realized that despite the brevity of time he'd known Noreen, their relationship had gone deeper than any he'd been in since Valerie's death. And he owed her an explanation of some kind.

As he drove to her house, he tried to figure out just what kind of explanation to use. He didn't want to lie to her, nor did he want to tell her the truth.

His tragedy was his own, and he'd learned a long time ago that sharing that tragedy only brought up more complications. He wanted...needed to keep it separate…guard it like a secret mantra that would keep him safe from any stupid future mistakes.

He pulled into Noreen's driveway, wondering what sort of reception he might encounter from her. Anger? Coldness? He deserved whatever he got.

Billy greeted him at the front door, in his face a child's delighted welcome. ''Hey, sport, where's your mom?''

''She's working in the backyard planting flowers and stuff.''

''How come you're not helping her?'' Vinnie asked.

Billy frowned. ''She's kind of cranky today so I'm watching cartoons instead.'' The little boy captured Vinnie's hand in his. ''Wanna see my room?''

Vinnie hesitated. What he wanted to do was get this over with, apologize to Noreen and forget about her and this little boy with his copper hair, sunshine smile and open, loving heart.

''Come on. I got stuff I want to show you.''

Before Vinnie could protest, Billy pulled him down the hall and through the first doorway. Vinnie entered the messy, chaotic world of a little boy, complete with the scent of bubblegum, sweaty socks and cedar shavings.

''Look,'' Billy said, tugging Vinnie over to a dresser top covered with a variety of treasures. ''This is a rock I got that shines in the sun, and this is a pinecone that a squirrel tried to eat.'' He pulled Vinnie away from the dresser and to the nightstand. On top of it was a small cage. ''This is my hamster,

Richard. You can't see him now 'cause he hides during the day.''

"If you have a hamster, then what do you need a baby for?" Vinnie asked teasingly.

Billy frowned and sat down on the edge of the brown plaid spread that covered the bed. "A hamster's not like a baby. Richard doesn't blow bubbles with his mouth or talk or do anything that's really fun. A hamster can't be a brother or a sister, and that's what I want.''

He jumped up off the bed and grabbed Vinnie's hand once again. "Look over here...I got pictures that I drewed in school hanging on the wall. That's a dinosaur and that's an airplane.''

The pictures looked surprisingly alike to Vinnie, but he nodded solemnly, touched that Billy obviously wanted to impress him, to share his little world with him.

"Look," Billy raced back to the side of the bed and picked up the flashlight Vinnie had bought for him. "I keep it right next to me at night, and if I wake up and it's too dark, I turn it on." He set the light down, then raced back to Vinnie and threw his arms around Vinnie's waist. "Thanks for getting it for me.''

Vinnie closed his eyes, steeling himself against the utter trust and love the little boy offered so freely. He patted Billy on the back, then moved away. "I really need to go talk to your mom now. Why don't you go back and watch the rest of your cartoons?''

"Okay. Maybe you could come back in later and I'll show you how I can do a card trick.''

"We'll see," Vinnie said as they walked back into the living room. With Billy back on the sofa, instantly engrossed in the cartoons again, Vinnie went into the kitchen and looked out the window.

Noreen was at the very back of the yard, facing away from the house. She sat on the ground at the edge of a flower bed, pulling weeds with a vengeance. He wondered if she imagined each weed held his face. He drew a deep breath, then stepped out the back door.

Apparently she didn't hear his approach for she continued her work as he walked across the lawn toward her. It wasn't until he drew close enough that his shadow fell across her that she jumped up and whirled around in surprise.

For a brief moment he saw raw pain in her eyes, pain he knew he'd placed there. In the blink of an eye it was gone, her gaze frosty instead. "What are you doing here?"

"I've come to apologize."

"For standing me up?" She shrugged. "It's no big deal. Don't worry about it. I don't want an apology."

She started to turn back around but he stopped her, placing his hands on her shoulders. "It is a big deal," he countered. "And I need to apologize." He tried to hold her gaze, but she averted hers from him, instead staring off to the side.

"Okay. I accept your apology." She looked at him again, a touch of defiance in her gaze. "Jeez, Vinnie, it was just a date."

Her flippant words ached inside him, because he

knew they weren't true. "It was more than that, and I know it."

She jerked out of his grasp. "So, what do you want, Vinnie?" Tears sparkled on her eyelashes, each sparkle shooting a shaft of pain through him. "You want to hear me tell you I'm in love with you. Okay. I love you. You won whatever perverse game it is for you."

"It's not a game, Noreen. It's never been a game," he protested. He raked a hand through his hair and sank down to the ground. "Things just got out of control. We were just supposed to have fun. Nobody was supposed to get hurt."

"Surprise, surprise. I guess you underestimated the strength of your own charm," she replied. "Don't feel responsible, Vinnie. I'm the one who made the mistake. You were never anything but honest with me."

Even now, knowing he had no intentions of continuing a relationship with her, there was nothing more he wanted than to gather her into his arms and kiss away the tears that still clung like diamonds to her eyes.

He realized at that moment he cared too much for her, owed her nothing less than the truth. "I had to leave town yesterday. I needed to go to Chicago and place flowers on the graves of my wife and daughter."

Noreen stared at him in surprise. Of all the reasons she'd imagined him coming up with for standing her up, this one certainly hadn't entered her mind. "What?" She moved closer to him, her own pain forgotten as she saw the torment in his eyes.

"Yesterday was the two-year anniversary of my wife and daughter's deaths."

"Oh, Vinnie." She reached for him, then stopped, sensing he didn't want her comfort and feared her pity. "What happened?" she asked softly.

He sighed, a sound as forlorn as a cold winter wind. "My wife, Valerie, and I bickered all day with each other, one of those times when we fought about nothing really important but were just on each other's nerves. Valerie was mad because I spent most of the day cooped up in my office working. At that time I was a lawyer and working on a big case. I was irritated with her for not understanding how important the case was to me."

He frowned and drew a deep breath, as if needing to tap into some inner strength to continue. "By the time night came, we were so at odds that I decided to sleep on the sofa downstairs, leaving Valerie alone in our bed upstairs and Melanie sleeping in her room." He closed his eyes, his features pale and twisted in grief.

Noreen wanted to tell him to stop, that he didn't have to tell her, didn't have to put himself through this torment just to explain a stupid broken date to her.

"Later the authorities discerned the fire started between the floors...faulty wiring." He gazed up into the sky, squinting against the late-afternoon sun. "I came to briefly in the house, just enough to know we were all in trouble. The firemen managed to save me. I was the only one they could save." The last words echoed with a bitter ring.

Again Noreen fought the impulse to pull him into her arms. "Is that why you decided to become a fireman?"

He nodded. "I watched them do everything in their power to get to Valerie and Melanie in time. When they weren't successful, I saw the pain of failure in their eyes, the mourning they did for my wife and child."

This time Noreen didn't fight her impulse. She scooted closer to him and placed an arm around his neck in comfort. "Oh, Vinnie, why didn't you tell me this before?" It made so many things clear to her…those dark shadows in his eyes, his need to keep things on the surface.

He shrugged. "I didn't want your pity. Besides, it's over. It's in the past."

Yes, it was in his past. Just like Jesse was in her past. And even though Jesse's betrayals could in no way compare to the death of Vinnie's family, the end result was the same. She'd been betrayed by Jesse. Vinnie had been betrayed by fate, leaving behind a reluctance to trust again. A reluctance to believe happily ever after was possible.

But Vinnie had made her realize there was life after loss. He'd made her want to trust again, love again. Wasn't it possible he was in the same place as she was…on the verge of learning to love again? All she had to do was make him realize happiness could happen twice in a lifetime.

For a long moment they remained seated, Noreen's arm around his neck. They didn't talk. She simply hung on to him while he slowly, resolutely placed the past back where it belonged...in the past.

"I'd better get home," he finally said, although he seemed reluctant to move.

"You don't have to go. You could stay here...eat dinner with us, maybe spend the night." He turned and looked at her in surprise. She felt the blush that stole across her cheeks, but she held his gaze resolutely.

"Why, Noreen Simmons, that sounds like a proposition to me."

"It is," she agreed, her face flaming hotter.

Nothing he'd said to her had changed her feelings for him. In truth, knowing about his past anguish only deepened her love for him. And she couldn't believe that he didn't feel something for her. "Vinnie, you told me it was time to get on with my life, and that's what I want to do...with you." She held her breath as a pained expression crossed his features.

He stood, then pulled her to her feet. Gently, tenderly he cupped her face with his hands, his eyes revealing his deep regret. "I can't, Noreen. I can't see you anymore. I can't be around you anymore. I'm sorry I let things go so far between us, but I'm not the man you need in your life. I just can't risk it again. I just can't love you." He dropped his hands and turned and walked away.

Noreen watched him until his image shimmered and blurred with her tears. She'd believed she knew all the ways a heart could break, but she'd been wrong. As she watched him walk out of her yard, out of her life, she discovered a new way, and she wasn't at all sure this heartbreak would ever mend.

The alarm rang at six o'clock on the next Friday night, sending the firemen into instant action. Within seconds the fire engine was on its way to Third and Oak, where an apartment building blazed out of control.

Vinnie hadn't been on duty, but had been at the station just wasting time...something he'd done a lot of in the past week since breaking it off with Noreen.

He had no desire to date, no interest in spending time with any other woman. After Valerie's death, it had taken months for her features to start to dim in his mind. He wondered how long it would be before Noreen's finally faded.

When the alarm went off and the dispatcher stated she was calling in all volunteers and off-duty firemen, Vinnie jumped into his gear and got into his car. Slapping the whirling red light and siren on his roof, he followed behind the fast-moving fire truck to the scene of the fire.

He smelled it before he saw it...the acrid, smoke scent of destruction. A black column swirled skyward, and although he was still a block away, the air was filled with flying soot and thick smoke.

Vinnie's hands tightened on the steering wheel, slick with damp perspiration as dread billowed inside him. An apartment building...that meant people in jeopardy.

When the burning structure came into view, Vinnie

parked his car and hit the sidewalk at a run, knowing every second counted when it came to saving lives.

The street directly in front of the building was clogged with people, making it difficult for the fire truck to get through. Horn blaring, sirens screeching, inch by inch the lumbering vehicle approached.

"My baby," a woman cried, tears streaming down her face. "He's still on the second floor. Please, somebody save my little Benny." Her gaze connected with Vinnie's and her despair, her anguish touched a memory inside him, the memory of those same pleas on his lips, that same anguish ripping out his guts.

Without hesitation Vinnie ran for the front door of the blazing building.

"Pastorelli! Wait! Stop!"

Vinnie was vaguely aware of the chief's voice, but he ignored it, knowing only that he had to save Benny. He entered a smoke-darkened foyer, the elevator to the right, the stairs to the left.

Intense heat assailed him as he took the stairs, the air growing thicker…darker with every step. He tried to breath shallowly, cursing the impulse that had sent him racing in without all the proper equipment.

He reached the second floor, the heat nearly unbearable and the smoke so dark, so thick he could barely see. "Benny!" he cried as he crashed through one of the two apartment doors. He wondered if the kid was old enough to know he was in danger…if the smoke had already gotten to him so much that he was in no condition to reply to Vinnie's cry.

He lowered himself to his hands and knees, crawling near the floor where the smoke wasn't as thick.

His eyes burned, and he coughed again and again as his lungs attempted to expel the noxious air he breathed.

It took him only minutes to check the first apartment. No child. He had to get to the next apartment. He had to save Benny.

In the hallway he collapsed with a spasm of coughing, light-headed as he rubbed his tearing eyes. He had to…he had to save…he had to save Valerie and Melanie. He shook his head…no, that wasn't right. Benny. He had to save Benny.

Confusion swirled in his head along with the smoke and heat that surrounded him. Valerie. Melanie. Where were they? Why couldn't he find them, save them?

"Pastorelli." The faint, disembodied voice came from the nearby stairwell.

"Here," Vinnie called, recognizing the voice as belonging to Sam.

Sam appeared through the smoke, a lumbering figure in an asbestos suit and hood. He approached Vinnie and knelt next to him. "What are you trying to do? Be a dead hero?" he said as he grabbed Vinnie's shoulders and helped him up.

"Don't worry about me," Vinnie exclaimed. "I'm okay. Just find the kid. Find Benny."

"There is no kid," Sam replied. "Come on, let's get you out of here."

Together the two men stumbled back down the stairs, dodging falling, burning ceiling tiles and flying glass. Sam half supported, half dragged Vinnie out of the building and to a grassy area next door where an ambulance awaited anyone needing medical treatment.

Vinnie didn't fight the paramedic who slapped an oxygen mask over his face and forced him to lie down. He still felt woozy and light-headed and knew a few minutes of breathing the clean air would help clear the confusion from his head.

"Are you all right?" The woman who'd been crying looked at Vinnie anxiously. An ugly, bald little dog yapped from the cradle of her arms. Vinnie nodded, and she gave him a smile of relief. "Oh, I'm so glad. When I got outside and didn't see Benny here...I just panicked and thought he was still inside."

Vinnie stared at her. A dog. Benny hadn't been a child but a dog. And if he'd taken half a minute to find out the facts, he'd never have risked not only his own life, but the lives of his fellow officers as well.

As the woman walked away, he ripped the oxygen mask from his face. He raked a hand through his hair and sat up, head in his hands as his mind worked with shining clarity.

He hadn't gone into that burning building to save Benny. He'd gone in to save Valerie and Melanie. For the past eighteen months, he'd been on a futile quest to change history, save two lives that couldn't be saved.

Like Noreen and her father, clinging to each other, Vinnie had been clutching the past, trying to change what couldn't be altered.

Bad things happen to good people. He'd said those words to Noreen but hadn't embraced them himself.

Valerie and Melanie's deaths had been tragic accidents, and while his heart would always retain a place for them, his heart was now open to hope.

And with the wealth of hope that flowed through him, his thoughts turned to Noreen. Noreen and Billy. What fate had taken from him, it now offered back...different, but just as wonderful. He was a man without a family. And they were a family without a man.

He got up, still a little woozy, but waved away the paramedic. "I'm fine," he assured the young woman.

The fire was out and the firemen were draining hoses to be reeled and attending to the other tasks that signaled the end of a job. Vinnie started over to help, but stopped in his tracks as he saw the chief approaching him, his features a thundercloud of anger. Vinnie steeled himself for the coming storm, knowing he deserved whatever he was about to receive.

"I should fire your butt for a stunt like that," Charlie shouted angrily. "You know better than to race into a burning building unprepared. You not only put yourself at risk, but you put Sam at risk as well."

"You're absolutely right. It was a stupid thing to do," Vinnie agreed. "I'm sorry, Chief. It will never happen again."

His humble apology apparently both surprised and defused Charlie's anger. He frowned and raked a hand through his hair in irritation. "Go home, Vinnie," he finally said. "The fire is out, and you aren't even officially on duty. Go home and we'll talk about this tomorrow."

"There's nothing to talk about," Vinnie countered with respect. "It will never happen again because I'm giving you my two-week notice. I'm quitting the department."

Charlie's eyebrows raised so high they threatened to jump off his forehead. "Vinnie, you're overwrought, probably suffering some kind of smoke stupidness. We'll talk about it in the morning."

Vinnie grinned. "No, Charlie, not smoke stupidness. The smoke has finally cleared from my head, and for the first time in a long while I'm thinking incredibly smart." He backed away from Charlie, flashed him a parting grin, then raced for his car.

Chapter Twelve

"More wine?" Bobby Sanford smiled at Noreen across the restaurant table.

"No, thanks, I'm fine," Noreen forced an answering smile, unable to believe that she was having dinner with Bobby Sanford with his plaid socks and lime-scented cologne.

It had been the longest week of Noreen's life. She hadn't realized how much Vinnie had filled her days until he was no longer there.

Each morning she awakened and for a moment forgot that he'd turned his back on her love, turned his back on any chance for happiness they might have together. And in those brief moments of forgetfulness, her heart swelled with her love for him, and her mind taunted her with visions of what might have been.

Reality always returned, slamming into her with the force of a truck against her chest. She'd cried enough tears to flirt with dehydration, tried to forget each and every moment she'd ever spent with Vinnie Pastorelli.

It had been Cindy's idea that she go out with Bobby, urging Noreen not to crawl back in the shell she'd been in before Vinnie had entered her life. Noreen had agreed...reluctantly.

The past seven days had been particularly lonely as Charlie had spent most of his free time at the hospital visiting Emily. Noreen was thrilled that her matchmaking attempt appeared to be a big success, but she hadn't considered the void that would be left when her father stopped his pop-in visits.

"It's been a beautiful summer so far, hasn't it?" Bobby commented, his voice stilted and overly formal.

"Yes, it has." She stirred her spaghetti with her fork, wanting nothing more than for the earth to open and swallow her up. It had taken only minutes of conversation to discern that she and Bobby Sanford had absolutely nothing in common.

"So, how's the used-car business?" she asked, trying to find some sort of connection that would help pass the time until they could call it a night...and a failure.

"Terrific," he said with more enthusiasm than he'd shown thus far. "Why? You in the market? I've got a sweet little Chevy down on the lot. I could cut you one heck of a deal."

Noreen smiled apologetically. "I really don't need another car."

"Oh, okay."

A commotion at the restaurant entrance made them

both turn and look. A gasp escaped Noreen as she saw Vinnie coming toward her. Clad in his yellow work slicker and hat, his face streaked with grime and soot, he looked as out of place in the elegant surroundings as a June bug on a snow drift.

As he stopped at their table, she rose, fear shooting through her. "Vinnie...what is it? Is it my dad?" Why else would he be here still clad in work clothes?

"No, your dad is fine. Everyone is fine," he hurriedly assured her.

Relief fluttered through her. "Then what are you doing here?"

"I need to talk to you."

Noreen gazed at him coolly, although her heart thudded more rapidly. "How did you know I was here?"

"I stopped by your house. Cindy told me where to find you."

What was he doing? Playing more games? He'd already told her all there was to say. He couldn't love her. End of subject. "I'm busy right now, Vinnie." She sat back down and smiled at Bobby.

Vinnie didn't move. Noreen picked up her fork and once again stirred her spaghetti, all too conscious of his nearness. Even beneath the heavy scent of smoke that clung to him, she could smell a whisper of his familiar cologne. Her heart constricted painfully in response.

"Just tell me one thing, Noreen." His voice was low, deep and so damned sexy.

She dropped her fork and looked back at him once again. "What?"

He jabbed a finger in Bobby's direction. "Is there a possibility that this is Mr. Right?"

Pride made her hesitate. She wanted to say yes. She wished she could say maybe, but either answer would be a lie. "No." The single word whispered out of her with regret.

Vinnie's eyes gleamed darkly. "Then come outside and talk to me." He grinned, the achingly handsome smile that sent an arrow through her heart. "I promise to make it worth your while."

"I've grown immune to the power of your charming sweet talk," she replied. She didn't want to hear what he had to say, feared her heart couldn't stand another go round with him.

"Uh...is there a problem here?" Bobby asked hesitantly.

"No, there's no problem," Noreen said, delivering a scathing glare to Vinnie.

He grinned. "You sure I can't charm you into a moment of your time?"

"Positive," she replied firmly.

"Then I guess I'll have to resort to caveman tactics." She gasped as he pulled her up from her chair and in one smooth movement bent her over one of his shoulders in a traditional fireman carry.

"Put me down," Noreen cried, aware of the amused and interested stares of the diners they passed as he carried her toward the front door.

"In a minute," he agreed, his voice irritatingly pleasant.

What was he up to? Noreen wondered. What was he doing here, face covered with smoke and eyes lit with flames? She thought about fighting him, beating on his back and kicking her feet until he set her down, but she knew it would only make a bigger spectacle.

He didn't put her down until they left the restaurant and walked out into the warm night air. "You look like hell," she said when he released her next to his car.

He laughed. "Always a straight shooter."

"Where was the fire?"

"An apartment building on Oak. Everyone got out all right, although the building suffered quite a bit of damage. And that's what I want to talk to you about."

"What? The apartment fire?" She hadn't realized there'd been any kind of hope in her heart until that moment, when it whooshed out of her with a sigh.

She turned away from him, not wanting him to see the disappointment in her eyes, to see that she was still a fool for him. "What is this about? A volunteer effort to help the residents of the apartment building? You know I'll do whatever I can to help."

"Noreen..." He stepped behind her and placed his hands on her shoulders. "About last week...about us."

She closed her eyes, grateful that her back remained to him as a sudden thought occurred to her. "Is my father giving you a hard time? I didn't say anything to him...but maybe he heard something through the grapevine...."

He laughed. "Your father won't be giving me a hard time on the job anymore...I quit the department."

She whirled around in surprise. "You what?"

"I quit. As of about an hour ago."

"But...but why?" She searched his face, seeking answers beneath the soot streaks. "Did...did something happen?"

He swept his hat off his head and placed it on the hood of his car. "Yeah, something happened." For the first time the levity that had lightened his eyes faded, replaced by a deep emotion she'd never seen before. He looked away, past her and to some indiscernible place in the distance. "I did something really stupid this evening. I went in a fire unprepared and unequipped, forcing the chief to send another man in after me."

Noreen said nothing, knowing the seriousness of what he'd just confessed.

"It wasn't the first time I'd done something like that," he said. "But this time I realized what I was doing...chasing phantoms from my past and attempting to change a history that can't be changed." He raked a hand through his hair and laughed wryly. "Hell, I'm not a fireman, I'm a lawyer, and it's time I get back to what I do best."

"If that's what you want, Vinnie, then I'm happy for you." And she was. Despite her own heartache where he was concerned, she wanted his happiness...even if it didn't include her.

He drew close to her, so close they almost touched. "I went into that fire today as a man afraid to let go of the past, afraid of what hurt the future might bring. The thought of falling in love again terrified me." He reached a finger up and lightly traced the curve of her jaw. "And in that apartment building I didn't face the blaze of the fire, rather I faced myself and all my weaknesses. And you're my strongest weakness, Noreen. I realized it was too late to shield my heart from you and Billy. You were already there, inside of me, and I know I don't want to spend the rest of my life without you."

Noreen gazed at him uncertainly. "Oh, Vinnie, please tell me you haven't suddenly decided at this moment to exhibit a perverse sense of humor."

He smiled, the gentle but sexy smile she loved, only this time it was filled with such promise it stole her breath away. "My love, I would never joke about anything as serious as the rest of my life with you."

"Are you sure?" she asked breathlessly, afraid to hope, afraid to believe what he seemed to be offering her.

"I've never been more sure about anything in my life." He pulled her into his arms. "Life is too short to waste it being afraid." He shook his head ruefully. "I knew I was a goner the first day I saw those cute freckles dancing on your shoulders."

He gave her no chance to reply, but instead covered her lips with his, kissing her with a sweet passion, a promise of forever she'd never tasted before.

"Marry me, Noreen," he said when he broke the kiss. "Marry me and let's give Billy the little brother or sister he wants. Marry me and grow old with me."

"Be an old married couple and fight over the blankets at night?" she teased, loving him with every breath she drew.

"I'll let you have the blankets," he said, no responding humor in his eyes. "I...I know I hurt you last week, and I'll spend the rest of my life making it up to you.''

"Shhh." She placed a finger on his lips. "The only thing you have to do is promise to love me every day for the rest of your life."

"That's easy. Does this mean you'll marry me?" His gaze held hers intently, as if he feared she might say no.

"Oh, Vinnie, how can you even think I wouldn't. I love you and yes...yes, I'll marry you."

He claimed her lips once again in a kiss that bared his heart and touched her soul. A kiss that she knew was only the beginning of their glorious future together.

Without tears, the soul would know no rainbows. That's what he'd told her the night Emily was ill. As she gazed into Vinnie's eyes, felt the love that radiated from him, she knew she'd finally found her rainbow.

"Noreen, honey. Can I come in?"

Noreen opened her bedroom door to admit her father. "Is it time?" she asked, nervously sliding her palms down the front of her pale pink silk dress.

"Almost. I just wanted to talk to you for a minute." Charlie shifted from foot to foot, obviously uncomfortable in the somber suit he wore. His blue eyes gazed at her for a long moment. He smiled and shook his head. "You look beautiful. I wish your mama was here to share this day with us."

"She is, Dad. She's here in spirit." Noreen hugged her father, noting that as usual his hair stood askew.

She reached up and finger combed it back into place. "And you look very handsome, far too young to be the father of the bride."

Charlie snorted. "I look like an old fool in a monkey suit. Emily helped me pick out the tie."

Noreen straightened the knot at his neck. "And it's a very nice tie."

"Quit fussing over me, I got something to say to you." Charlie took a step back from her, and Noreen eyed him curiously. His brow was wrinkled, as if whatever he had to say weighed heavy inside him.

"What is it, Dad?" She carefully sat on the edge of the bed.

"I was wrong about Pastorelli." The words blurted out of him with force.

Noreen hid a smile, knowing how difficult it was for Charlie O'Roark to admit he was wrong about anything. She remained silent as he paced back and forth in front of her.

"I knew right off there was something happening between you and him. That first day when you met him your eyes sparkled like I'd never seen before." He stopped his pacing and looked at Noreen. "And it scared me. Scared me because I thought if you got involved with somebody I'd end up all alone." Misery filled his face. "For four years I didn't want you to find anyone because I was a selfish, frightened old man."

"Oh, Dad." Noreen stood and hugged him once again. "If you were selfish, then so was I. I needed you as much as you needed me." She smiled at him. "You've always been a giving, loving father, and I'm always going to need you in my life. Marrying Vinnie doesn't change wanting you to be a part of our life, of our family.''

He nodded and cleared his throat. ''He's a good man,'' he said gruffly. ''And if he ever decides he's finished with this lawyering idea, he's got a place at the department.'' Charlie's eyes gleamed with humor. ''Big Red hasn't been as nicely polished since he quit.''

Noreen laughed. It had been a little over a month since Vinnie had quit the fire department and proposed to her. In that month he'd rented a small office on Main Street and hung a shingle announcing his new position as attorney.

His new office wasn't all the past month had brought. The love that he had recognized on the night of the flaming apartment building had only flourished and grown with the passing of time. Vinnie, finally putting his past behind, had embraced the future and his wife and son to be, with a fervor and passion that promised a lifetime of love. And Noreen returned that promise, knowing this was the man she wanted to grow old with…the man her heart and her head told her was Mr. Right.

''Come on, honey,'' Charlie said, interrupting her thoughts. ''I can hear the music, so it's time.''

It's time. Time to walk out of the bedroom and out the back door where neighbors and friends awaited her. Time to stand before the minister and profess her love for Vinnie. Time to say the vows that would unite them forever in a bond of love and commitment.

Noreen's heart swelled with emotion as her father

led her out the back door and across the lawn toward the white canopy that had been erected for the ceremony. Vinnie stood tall and handsome, that crazy, sexy smile curving his lips as he watched her approach. Billy stood next to Vinnie, his red hair glistening in the sunlight and a wide grin decorating his face. Charlie gave her hand to Vinnie, then moved to stand on the other side of Billy.

Her three men. The three who held her heart. Vinnie squeezed her hand, and she focused on him, tears of happiness springing to her eyes. This man. This gorgeous, sexy, wonderful man. He looked at her with those dark eyes of his, promising days of laughter, nights of passion. She'd finally found the man beneath the shallow flirting, and it was the man she loved.

As the minister performed the ceremony, Noreen's gaze remained focused on Vinnie. Happiness she'd never known blossomed inside her as they solemnly said the vows that bound them to one another through eternity.

"I now pronounce you man and wife," the minister finished.

"Now are you guys gonna make me a baby?" Billy's voice quipped in the moment of silence that followed the minister. The crowd erupted in laughter and claps as Vinnie nodded his head, then pulled his new bride into his arms for a kiss that sealed their future.

Epilogue

"Vinnie...it's time." Noreen spoke softly, fighting the waves of labor that had begun two hours before. At first, the pains were irregular but now they were spaced five minutes apart and she knew the baby she carried was eager to make its entrance into the world.

Vinnie murmured and turned over on his side, his even breathing letting her know he was still sound asleep.

She touched his shoulder, and his eyes flew open.

His dark gaze caressed her lovingly, then his eyes widened with awakeness and he sat up. "Did you say it's time?"

She nodded and giggled as he grabbed his jeans from the foot of the bed and tried to get into them before standing. Dressed, he helped her up. "Go wake Billy. While you get him dressed, I'll get ready. Oh...and call Dad. He'll want to be there."

"Are you sure you're all right?" Vinnie frowned

worriedly as she caught her breath and sank to the edge of the bed.

She managed to nod, the pain growing more intense than it had been moments before. "We'd better hurry," she finally managed to gasp.

Vinnie whirled out of the room as if the fires of hell nipped at his feet. Love for her husband welled up inside her, momentarily easing the pain of her contraction.

The last year of being Mrs. Vinnie Pastorelli had been a fantasy come true for Noreen. Vinnie was not only passionate and loving, but also gentle and thoughtful...a perfect husband for her, and a perfect daddy for Billy. No longer a fireman, Vinnie had opened a law office and seemed content once again being a lawyer.

As she dressed, she heard Vinnie rousing Billy from sleep, then her son's excited voice as he realized it was almost time for his baby brother or sister to arrive.

Moments later they were in the car heading for the hospital. Noreen found it difficult to focus on anything but the pains, which were coming closer and closer together.

"It's going to be a baby brother, isn't it, Mommy?" Billy asked. "I really, really want a baby brother."

"We'll have to wait and see, honey," Noreen replied. They had agreed not to learn the sex of the baby before the birth, although both Vinnie and Noreen had tried to prepare Billy for the possibility of a sister.

As they pulled up before the emergency entrance at the hospital, they heard the wail of a siren coming closer. Before Vinnie could help Noreen out of the car, pumper Big Red came into view, lights flashing and siren blaring. When the fire truck had come to a full stop, Charlie jumped off and raced toward them.

"Honey, are you all right?" Charlie bumped shoulders with Vinnie as they both attempted to help her out of the car. Again Noreen's heart expanded. How she loved the men in her life.

"Grandpa, we didn't need the firemen," Billy said as they all hurried toward the hospital entrance. "Firemen don't bring babies." His voice held the grown-up knowledge he'd learned. "Vinnie does."

Their laughter rang in Noreen's heart as she was whisked away on a stretcher.

Exactly four hours and twenty minutes later, Vinnie left the delivery room, pausing in the corridor to wipe away tears of joy. He'd once believed he'd never know happiness again, but he'd been wrong. Noreen and Billy filled his heart with love and gladness, and now he had a new baby to add to his overflow of happiness.

He knew there would be times when he'd remember the woman and the little girl he'd lost. They would always hold a piece of his heart, a special place in his memory.

He drew a deep breath and walked into the waiting room where Charlie sat with a sleepy Billy on his lap.

But once Billy realized Vinnie was back in the waiting room with them, he jumped up and asked anxiously, "Do I have a baby brother?"

Vinnie took Billy's hand. "Why don't you come with me and let's see." Vinnie gestured for Charlie to follow.

Noreen sat up in the hospital bed, the newborn baby in her arms. Her face glowed, and Vinnie knew it was an image he would forever carry in his heart.

Billy approached the side of the bed and peered at the baby, a frown furrowing his forehead. "Is it a baby boy or a baby girl?" he asked.

"A boy," Noreen said and smiled. "You finally have your baby brother."

Billy nodded, but his frown didn't ease. "He's awful little." Billy looked at his mom. "Is he supposed to be that little?"

She nodded and he sighed.

"I guess he won't be able to play catch for a while."

The baby fussed, a mewling noise that drew Billy even closer. "Hey, don't cry. Don't cry, little brother. I'm going to take care of you. We're going to be buddies...you and me and our daddy." Billy looked at Vinnie shyly. "Can I call you my daddy, too?"

Raw emotion choked in Vinnie's throat. He nodded, and wondered what he had done to deserve this woman and her son.

"Well...what are you going to call this bundle of joy?" Charlie asked, his eyes suspiciously glassy. "We can't very well just call him Billy's baby brother."

"We thought we'd call him Charles," Noreen said. "Charles O'Roark Pastorelli."

Her father blinked once...then again...obviously overcome with emotion.

Vinnie laughed and clapped his father-in-law on the back. "I've been waiting a long time to see you speechless," he said with a laugh.

"Maybe a baby sister wouldn't be a bad idea," Billy quipped. "Then me and little Charlie would be big brothers to her. What do you think? Mom? Dad?"

Suddenly they were all laughing. Vinnie lifted Billy in his arms. "We'll practice on little Charlie, then talk about a baby sister in a year or so...deal?"

"Deal," Billy agreed.

Vinnie placed Billy back on the floor, then leaned over and kissed Noreen. "I love you," he whispered.

Love circled around him, filled him up, shot warmth through him as she smiled.

"I love you, too."

* * * * *

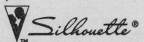

Take 2 bestselling love stories FREE

Plus get a FREE surprise gift!

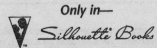

HE CAN CHANGE A DIAPER IN THREE SECONDS FLAT BUT CHANGING HIS MIND ABOUT MARRIAGE MIGHT TAKE SOME DOING! HE'S ONE OF OUR

Fabulous Fathers

July 1998
ONE MAN'S PROMISE by Diana Whitney (SR#1307)
He promised to be the best dad possible for his daughter. Yet when successful architect Richard Matthews meets C. J. Moray, he wants to make another promise—this time to a wife.

September 1998
THE COWBOY, THE BABY AND THE BRIDE-TO-BE by Cara Colter (SR#1319)
Trouble, thought Turner MacLeod when Shayla Morrison showed up at his ranch with his baby nephew in her arms. Could he take the chance of trusting his heart with this shy beauty?

November 1998
ARE YOU MY DADDY? by Leanna Wilson (SR#1331)
She hated cowboys, but Marty Thomas was willing to do anything to help her son get his memory back—even pretend sexy cowboy Joe Rawlins was his father. Problem was, Joe thought he might like this to be a permanent position.

Available at your favorite retail outlet, only from

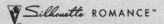

Silhouette ROMANCE™

Available October 1998
from Silhouette Books...

World's Most
Eligible Bachelors

DETECTIVE DAD
by Marie Ferrarella

The World's Most Eligible Bachelor: Undercover agent Duncan MacNeill, a wealthy heir with a taut body...and an even harder heart.

Duncan MacNeill just got the toughest assignment of his life: deliver a beautiful stranger's baby in the back seat of her car! This tight-lipped loner never intended to share his name with anyone—especially a mystery woman who claimed to have a total memory loss. But how long could he hope to resist succumbing to the lure of daddyhood—and marriage?

Each month, Silhouette Books brings you
a brand-new story about an absolutely
irresistible bachelor. Find out how the sexiest,
most sought-after men are finally caught.

Available at your favorite retail outlet.

Silhouette
ROMANCE™

COMING NEXT MONTH

#1318 THE GUARDIAN'S BRIDE—Laurie Paige
Virgin Brides
She was beautiful, intelligent—and too young for him! But
Colter McKinnon was committed to making sure Belle Glamorgan
got properly married. Still, how was he supposed to find her an
appropriate husband when all Colter really wanted was to make her
his bride?

**#1319 THE COWBOY, THE BABY AND THE
BRIDE-TO-BE—Cara Colter**
Fabulous Fathers
Handing over a bouncing baby boy to Turner MacLeod at his Montana
ranch was just the adventure Shayla Morrison needed. But once she got
a look at the sexy cowboy-turned-temporary-dad, she hoped her next
adventure would be marching down the aisle with him!

**#1320 WEALTH, POWER AND A PROPER WIFE
Karen Rose Smith**
Do You Take This Stranger?
Being the proper wife of rich and powerful Christopher Langston was
almost the fairy tale she had once dreamed of living. But sweet Jenny
was hiding a secret from her wealthy husband—and once revealed, the
truth could bring them even closer together...or tear them apart forever.

#1321 HER BEST MAN—Christine Scott
Men!
What was happening to her? One minute Alex Trent was
Lindsey Richards's best friend, and the next moment he'd turned into
the world's sexiest hunk! Alex now wanted to be more than friends—
but could he convince Lindsey to trust the love he wanted to give.

#1322 HONEY OF A HUSBAND—Laura Anthony
Her only love was back in town, and he had Daisy Hightower trembling
in her boots. For, if rugged loner Kael Carmody ever learned that her
son was also his, there would be a high price to pay...maybe even the
price of marriage.

#1323 TRUE LOVE RANCH—Elizabeth Harbison
The last thing Darcy Beckett wanted was to share her inherited ranch
with ex-love Joe Tyler for two months. But when Joe and his young
son showed up, the sparks started flying. Now Joe's son wants the two
months to go on forever...and so does Joe! Can he convince Darcy
they are the family she's always wanted?